# MAKE IT NYLONS

Joe P. Heggy, professional trouble-buster for an international construction firm, is travelling to Turkey. As the plane lands in Istanbul he looks out of the window and witnesses a murder — a man being stabbed. The victim was the leader of the country's Ultra-Nationalist Party. That glimpse of murder brings him trouble. Millions of fanatics try to pin the crime on him — his life is in danger. His only ally — an Amazonian Rumanian peasant with a passion for western nylons!

GORDON LANDSBOROUGH

# MAKE IT NYLONS

*Complete and Unabridged*

LINFORD
*Leicester*

First published in Great Britain

First Linford Edition
published 2010

British Library CIP Data

Landsborough, Gordon.
  Make it nylons. - - (Linford mystery library)
  1. Witnesses– –Fiction. 2. Mistaken identity
  - -Fiction. 3. Turkey- -Politics and government
  - -Fiction. 4. Suspense fiction.
  5. Large type books.
  I. Title II. Series
  823.9′14–dc22

  ISBN 978–1–44480–106–4

Published by
F. A. Thorpe (Publishing)
Anstey, Leicestershire

Set by Words & Graphics Ltd.
Anstey, Leicestershire
Printed and bound in Great Britain by
T. J. International Ltd., Padstow, Cornwall

This book is printed on acid-free paper

# 1

## I see it all

Right at the moment when the plane came in to land, a man was murdered below.

More, I saw it done.

We were coming in to the Istanbul airport, and floating over the sprawling, low buildings at a height of maybe sixty feet.

I was leaning across the Rumanian girl, looking out through the window and I saw it all happen.

I wasn't really interested in looking out and down, but it was a good excuse to get closer to that dame. I knew she liked it, anyway.

We'd been fixed in seats next to each other at Athens, and in that short two-three hour trip I learnt a lot about her.

She was an actress — the burlesque

kind. She sang and she danced and I guessed she had the figure that made everyone think she sang and danced well.

She was as ripe a piece of beauty as I've ever sat against in a plane. Rather tall, with black, wavy hair that had lights in it. And she had big, nearly black eyes that had lights in them too, and if ever nearly black eyes can have the green light hers had it.

All the way to Istanbul she had been giving me the come-hither. All the way she'd been smiling at Joe P. Heggy, and keeping her smiling face close to mine so that I didn't miss a thing about those curving, painted lips and those big, white, even teeth of hers. She was a wow, and Joe P. Heggy wasn't behind in accepting the come-hither.

We'd played kneesy-kneesy and footsy-wootsy for the last quarter of an hour and I knew things were going to be all right during the couple of weeks she was booked to appear in Istanbul. I told her the name of the hotel where I stayed, and I left it to her to fix up at the same place if she wanted to.

I was sure she wanted to.

So when we started coming in to land, I leaned across her, getting the scent of her soft perfumed body in the appreciative Heggy nostrils, and I had my arm across her warm, silk-covered shoulders. I was making a great play of showing her points around the airport, though I didn't know a damn thing about the place, anyway.

We were huddled close together, peering down through that airplane window, and enjoying every moment of close contact, when — I saw it happen.

But the girl didn't see it. I don't think she was looking at anything.

I saw those long, low, hutted buildings below me, and there was a black, shining car parked and I just caught the killer in the act. Between that black, shiny car and one of the buildings a man was stabbing into the back of another man.

It's amazing how clearly you see detail from a 'plane as it comes in to land. After all, we probably weren't moving at more than eighty or ninety miles an hour, and we weren't very high up above those buildings. Even those men didn't look such stumpy figures because we came at them from a low angle.

I saw for one fleeting instant a man unaware of death striking at him from the rear — a dumpy, oldish-looking man. And I saw a bigger, heavier man wearing a hat, striking upwards into the old man's back with a knife.

I also saw his face lift in the instant that he had struck and killed, startled by the sudden appearance of a roaring plane that floated above him.

Yeah, it's amazing what the eye can see and remember in detail all in a fraction of a second — if it wants to.

I was clawing out of my safety belt before we had touched down. The girl at my side was startled and was watching me in astonishment.

As I came out of that belt, I looked into her big, shining, near-black eyes and I rapped: 'Did you see it?'

But even as I asked the question I knew she couldn't have seen it or she wouldn't have been looking like that.

I looked round that plane and it was

apparent that I was the only witness to the crime. But that wasn't remarkable. In those twin-engined planes used on that service, nearly the only seats that get an unrestricted view of the ground below ways get a seat there for two reasons.

First, because there's less vibration in the rear of a plane, and secondly because those seats are right opposite the main door to the aircraft, and I like to be where I can get out of a plane easily if there's need for hurry. Joe P. Heggy has been in plane crashes before.

The British girl who was stewardess began to call out to me because I stood up while the plane was bumping along the ground. I took no heed of her. But I couldn't get out of the plane right away, not until the door was opened.

I was first out, and I hadn't wasted the half-minute before they'd got the passenger steps trollied up to the plane door. I'd given a swift explanation to that Rumanian girl. She didn't believe me, but she was prepared to look as if she did.

No one believed me after that. I got the entire airport running round in circles as

I ran, grip in hand, to the 'Passengers Out' door to the terminal building. I was shouting as I went in that I'd seen a man killed along by the airport buildings. I saw faces lift, Turkish faces, vaguely grey and colourless, with brown eyes that looked coldly, speculatively at me. They all registered, in the next instant, 'This fellow's crazy!'

The Immigration official thought I'd gone nuts, too, and when I tried to get past him he caught me by the arm and then a Turkish cop rushed up and held me. I got out of that grip by pulling out my American passport, and that released one arm because the Immigration officer used both hands to look at that passport.

I ripped my other arm free from the cop, dropped my grip and sprinted like heck down a passage and went out into the blazing sunshine. Behind me streamed dozens of agitated airport officials and several cops now. I wasn't behaving according to rule.

But I didn't give a damn about waiting for my passport to be stamped, and for my grip to be examined by the Customs.

I belted round the kiosks with their ices and candy displays, and then ran along the line of buildings in which the work of administration was done.

It seemed a long way to run, and I was streaming with sweat by the time I found the corpse. For he was a corpse. There wasn't a twitch of life left in that old boy.

There wasn't a sign of the murderer around either.

That's why I'd been running. In the hope of spotting the murderer before he could get away. Me, I don't like killers who sneak up behind and slip a knife into an unsuspecting victim's heart right under the lower rib.

The body was lying in the grey dust of that dirt road that backed the huts, He was sprawling flat on his face, his arms flung before him as if even in his dying moments he had tried to break that fall. His toes were turned in. I thought it made the corpse look comical and somehow it didn't seem decent to see a corpse with a trace of the comical about it.

But I didn't alter the position of those

feet. I didn't touch the body. It was for the police to come and do all that.

I just stood there and panted and sweated and looked round — and didn't see a thing. That black sedan that I had momentarily glimpsed wasn't there, and there wasn't even a dust cloud to tell where it had gone. But in those several minutes since the crime had been committed that car could have travelled a considerable distance.

At that moment the pack caught up with me. Fat men came trundling round a corner and their eyes lit up when they saw the crazy American standing there waiting to receive them. There was the Immigration officer waving my passport excitedly. Half the Customs were there, too, and there were other airport officials and they all looked very excited and very indignant because I'd made them run a long way.

The police were more decisive in their reactions at the sight of me. They saw the corpse and they saw me standing over it, so they grabbed me when they came up and they held me so that there was no chance of my getting away.

I didn't try to get away. I just kept yammering. 'For heaven's sake, get on a phone and tell them to stop a big black sedan that's just left the airport.'

No one seemed to understand English. Probably in their excitement no one wanted to understand English. And that was to the advantage of the murderer.

I got taken down to the main Istanbul police station after that, but that didn't worry me. I knew a police officer there — a big young fellow with more intelligence than you get in most cops. I told him my story and he knew that I was speaking the truth and he also knew that I couldn't have murdered that old boy. After all, how can a man in a landing aircraft slip a long, thin knife under the rib of a man sixty feet below him on the ground?

I went to my hotel, then. I wanted a shower and a change of clothing. It's not a good habit to start running on a hot Turkish afternoon.

There was a Customs official at the hotel when I arrived there. He'd brought my grip down for me, but he wouldn't surrender it until I'd paid a bill on some of the contents.

I paid it. Gladly.

Inside that grip were fifty pairs of best American nylons. Without those nylons Joe P. Heggy wasn't the man he could be with the local girls. For nylons can bring a smile to the face of any female in any country of the world.

I went up to my room. When I opened the door my foot kicked against an envelope. I looked down. There was a white envelope just inside the door. There had been a metallic clinking from within when my foot made contact with it.

I stooped and picked it up. It felt heavy, and I could feel some bulky metal object inside — it seemed there was more than one metal object because there was movement under the pressure of my fingers. I lifted the envelope to my nose. There was an odour of perfume attached to it.

The door from the tiny hallway of my apartment was open, so that I could look through into my room and even through the window which gave out on to the back of the hotel. I was standing there with that envelope to my nose, when my eyes flitted to that bright patch of light that was my window. Two silent men sat in silhouette against the window. Big men.

My fingers gripped the envelope tightly. My hands came down to my sides at once, and my hands were hard, balled-up fists.

Joe P. Heggy has been in enough trouble lately to make him suspicious of gents who sit silently inside an apartment that isn't theirs.

A voice said, sarcastically: 'The trouble-buster!'

I relaxed, hearing that voice. It was Marty Dooley's. Marty is one of the boys on this construction job that employs me. He is known as the Show Boss, because he is the guy who puts on top demonstrations of the Gissenheim dirt-shifters when the company goes out to pull in a big contract.

He's big and he's ginger and he's tough. We fight all the time, and yet we're friends.

11

With him was Tony Geratta. Think of a smiling Italian and you've got Tony, only he's not Italian, but a good East Side New Yorker. Tony is our Middle East sales representative.

I was among friends, though you wouldn't believe it, the way they talked to me.

Tony was grinning as big as they're made, and he was saying: 'Cripes, you're no trouble-buster. You're a troublemaker. Remind me to keep out of your life from now on.'

I went in and took a chair. I thought they wouldn't mind. After all, it was my apartment. I played around with that envelope, sniffing it, and speculating. And I was getting around to a few conclusions even before I opened it.

I thought I wouldn't open it while the boys were there. If it was what I thought it was, then life wouldn't be easy for me when they knew about it.

Marty, looking as Irish as any American ever looked, said: 'That thing dropped through your door a couple of minutes ago. We felt tired or we'd have opened it for you.'

Marty's eyes met mine. He'd got a suspicion about that envelope, too. He encouraged: 'Open it. Don't mind us, bub!'

I didn't open it. I sat and played with it in my hand and I thought of the possibilities it might open up to me — literally open up. For I knew now what was inside that envelope, and I could guess who had sent it.

I said, 'Let's get this right. This is my apartment — yeah?'

They nodded enthusiastic agreement.

I said, 'Then how come you're here ahead of me?'

Marty said, kindly, 'When we saw what was in the papers we thought we'd wait for you, to talk about it. We'd like your story at first hand. We guessed you wouldn't be long, so we tipped the floor servant to let us in to your room.' His hand waved. 'He knew we were friends.'

'He knows more than I do, then,' I growled, and the boys pretended to look shocked.

I looked at them. They could bring an awful lot of trouble on any man. And I wanted to get rid of them quickly, because of what I held in my hand, and yet there were things I wanted to know.

I asked, 'What did you see in the paper? And how long have you been able to read Turkish?'

They weren't going, so I peeled off my suit coat and started to drag myself out of a shirt that clung like a flypaper.

Tony flashed a bright smile and said, 'They got the afternoon editions — the special ones — down in the hotel lobby. Everyone got excited and the manager came across to speak to us about it.'

'About the murder out at the airport?'

'About that.'

The boys were looking at me very curiously. I got out of my pants. That gave them more to look at. I went across and fiddled with the shower and kept talking to them.

'You seem goddamned concerned about that murder?' For the moment I was more concerned about that envelope. If they'd go, I'd open it and see if my suspicions were correct.

Marty got up and he looked very big

and very American in his pansy Fifth Avenue suiting. And yet Marty was no pansy. He lit a cigarette and I saw those keen blue-green eyes under those rather shaggy ginger eyebrows staring at me where I stood under the spray.

'Joe, you lug, you don't seem to know what sort of a spot you're in — and Gissenheims, too.'

That startled me and brought my head from under the shower. I said, 'Come again?'

This time Marty came. 'The murdered man happened to be a mighty important man in Turkey — Habib Pasha.' I nodded. That young police officer had given me the name. 'He is — was — the head of the Ultra-Nationalist Party,' and I nodded at that too because I'd been told that also.

Marty lounged as near as he could get without catching the spray off my shoulders. His eyes were looking at that envelope.

He said, 'Are you dumber than usual, Joe? Don't you realise who the Ultra-Nationalists are — the UNP as they're known?'

I thought, the hell, right now I'm interested in that envelope and nothing else. But I answered, 'They're anti-American, anti-everything else. They're the isolationists of this part of the world. They want Turkey to remain aloof from the rest of the world's affairs and have nothing to do with any of the countries who might get into a war with each other.'

I got back under the shower, feeling pleased at the party-piece I had just delivered.

Then I saw Tony weighing that envelope in his hand, and I shot my head out from under the hissing water and rapped, 'You put that down, Tony, or else.'

Tony gave me a grin. He tossed the envelope back on to the table, and it made the dull clinking noise as of dissimilar metals knocking against each other. Tony said, 'I reckon I know what's inside there, Joe. Nice work — but see that it doesn't amount to more trouble for you.'

Tony was always on about that

trouble-busting job of mine. I was the guy who got shuffled around the world whenever Gissenheims ran into unusual problems that required a strong-arm boy's intervention. I had to go and bust up strikes and put down minor rebellions where they affected the Gissenheim worldwide interests.

But Tony always insists I make more trouble than ever I settle. That's Tony's idea. Sometimes I agree with it.

Marty said, 'Don't sidetrack, you two. This is goddamned serious.' I looked at Marty and realised that he was very serious, and for the first time I switched my brain on to this Habib Pasha murder to see how it could affect me and the Gissenheim projects here in Turkey.

Marty went right on talking. Plainly he had done a lot of thinking. 'There are two things that stick out a mile. Habib Pasha had been doing his damnedest to stop this United Nations work here in Turkey.'

That meant, principally, the construction of airfields with runways long enough to take the biggest bombers required to carry atom bombs. That was what

Gissenheim's were doing in Turkey — making airfields that all pointed towards a potential enemy who doesn't need to be named.

'Habib Pasha has a helluva lot of support in this country, and when a man is murdered, there is a tendency to make a martyr of him and his cause This probably means that the scale will be tipped in favour of the Ultra-Nationalists. They'll be more vociferous than ever. There was a hint in the paper that was read out to me that the Ultra-Nationalists, in fact, are already saying that Habib Pasha was slain by someone on the payroll of Uncle Sam.'

That brought me out of the shower. I stared at Marty. Then I exploded.

'It's damned nonsense,' I swore. And then I began to think. It doesn't matter where the truth lies, some politicians will fix a lie on to someone if it helps their cause even a fraction.

I started to towel. Marty was right, I was beginning to realise. The Ultra-Nationalists would declare this to be a political murder. Habib Pasha had been getting in the hair of the Americans; Habib Pasha gets killed and therefore it is logical, according to a political way of thinking, that the Americans inspired his death.

I looked over the towel at Marty and asked, 'You think they'll agitate to stop these United Nations' projects, here in Turkey?'

Marty nodded grimly. 'You bet your life they'll try. The thing is, I think they stand a good chance of succeeding. There is a lot of feeling in this country against Turkey being used as a military base by the United Nations. I'm betting that unless the real murderer of Habib Pasha becomes known, then we'll be told to stop any further work on those runways.'

That was serious. Gissenheim's had imported an enormous amount of dirt-shifting machinery and equipment, and if they didn't finish this contract they'd stand to lose a lot. I had a feeling that here was a job for the trouble-buster.

Tony was grinning over Marty's shoulder. It was the kind of smile you reserved for your best girl.

And I'm no lily. So I asked, sourly, 'What's hurting you, Tony?'

Tony flashed a gold tooth in an even bigger smile. He said, 'I reckon some newspaper editor doesn't like Americans, either. One American, anyway — Joseph Phineas Heggy.'

I didn't say anything, but started to climb into fresh clothing. I wanted to be ready just as soon as they'd finished their spiel, because there was an interesting time ahead for me — that envelope said so.

Tony lounged after me, and Marty was grinning tightly, as if enjoying a rather tough joke himself,

'They got your name in the paper attached to that murder, Joe. They put something in that paper that wasn't healthy from the Heggy point of view, I guess. They said that an American had witnessed the murder and had seen the face of the assassin!'

Tony wasn't smiling as he said that last sentence, and he was watching me to see if his words sank home.

They did.

'You think the murderer might try to remove the witness to his crime?'

Both boys nodded. I put something nice on my hair. I wanted to smell good.

Marty said, 'You're not up against an ordinary murderer, Joe. Don't kid yourself that way. The way we figure it, this is a political killing. Maybe some other political party had a grudge against Habib Pasha and thought they'd put him out of the way.'

Tony's voice came in softly at that. 'Or perhaps there's someone in the Ultra-Nationalist movement who wanted Habib Pasha out of the way! And maybe he figured Habib would be helping the Ultra-Nationalists more by being dead than alive.'

We both looked at Tony. Tony's a smart boy.

'You mean — ?'

'I mean, that the next head of the U.N.P. might be glad Habib went, no matter how he went. He'll be especially glad he went, for two reasons — one, because they can lay the crime at America's door, and secondly because he'll be the big shot now. That's all these politicians want, remember — to be the big shot.'

It was an interesting conjecture. But as far as I was concerned the only real point of significance was the idea that the political murderer might take a poke at Joe P. Heggy with the idea of silencing him. It makes a man think, when he realises he's maybe on a murder spot.

But I was still thinking about that envelope. I said, 'Boys, you interest me a lot. Now, go away and play for the next twenty-four hours I've work to do.'

Tony looked at the envelope and said, 'You call that work?'

I put on my quietest tie. I looked pretty when I stared at myself in the mirror. The boys weren't going. I looked hostile at them and slipped on my suit coat.

Marty gave a gingery smile. 'How come you came back to Istanbul so quickly, Joe? You only left for Athens with the boss yesterday.'

I got sore at that, remembering. 'Yeah, I left for Athens yesterday. The boss said there was urgent need for us both in

Greece. But, you know what, when I got to Athens I found why the boss had left Istanbul in a hurry.'

They looked mighty interested. The boss, so far as we're concerned is Berny Gissenheim — B.G. to the boys. He's a big fat slob, an introverted mass of uncertain humanity. He's got the heart of a chicken and all the time he tries to play the role of the big shot American business-tycoon. It doesn't kid the boys, though it kids other people.

The boys give the boss hell. The real boss is his father, old Gissenheim, now confined to a bath chair in distant Detroit. But Berny lives in terror of that rough-voiced old father of his, and goes into a sweat at the thought of being caught out over some damn fool thing or other.

The boys — not just Marty Dooley and Tony, but Dwight Laite, Gorby Tuhlman, Harry Sauer and others — know this and they've got a hold on the boss, and it's mighty useful for employees to be able to shove their boss around.

Sometime back G.B. made a slip-up

that would've cost the firm a quarter of a million dollars. The boys covered up the boss's mistake for, him, but ever since then we've blackmailed the slob, and the boss goes in fear and trembling of his assistants. It's the way all bosses should be.

I told them why B.G. had taken a powder out of Istanbul. 'He ran away from a woman.' I put all the contempt possible on my tongue at that. To Joe P. Heggy it wasn't reasonable that any man at any time should run away from a judy.

'Lav?'

I nodded. 'Lav,' I agreed. Lav was a frustrated, not-so-young Englishwoman known as Lavinia Dunkley. She'd lived a narrow, spinster life until just recently when she had inherited a bit of money and she'd come travelling abroad. She was a timid, trembling thing — until the moon came out. And then — wow!

Now, in her not-so-young years, she was suddenly trying to make up for all she had missed. She'd taken a yen for B.G. for her first passion, and she'd chased him all over Istanbul. And Berny was 'saving himself up for when the right woman came along.' He was that kind of sap.

She was half his size, and yet she had put the fear of death — a fate worse than death, even — into big, fat Berny. When it looked as if he was in peril, he'd ducked out and gone to Athens.

I didn't mind the boss getting the hell out of it, but what I did object to was being dragged away with him. For I'd met a piece of womanhood called Marie Konti, here in Istanbul, and I'd just been getting places with her when duty had flown me out to Athens.

'I was taken away just to keep him company,' I bellyached, the gripe still strong upon me. 'He took me away from a nice bit of homework, and for no good reason except that he's no man himself.'

The boys nodded in sympathy. They could appreciate my feelings. Tony asked me, in a kindly manner, 'What did Joe P. Heggy do then, when he'd found out the truth?' And he asked the question in the manner of a man who expects to hear that Joe P. Heggy had in fact done something pretty drastic about the matter.

I took a deep breath and then exploded, 'Goddamnit, what d'you think I did? I sent a telegram to little Lav in Berny's name inviting her to meet him in Athens.'

The boys nearly collapsed. They were picturing Berny's quivering fat face when he found himself confronted with little Lavinia Dunkley, who wanted to make up for wasted years.

But I still couldn't see anything to laugh about.

Marie Konti was lost to me, for by now she would be back in Ankara, and you know the harem-like kind of existence these girls lead even in Turkey today.

She was lost to me. The only consoling feature had been that lovely Rumanian girl in the plane. I could have forgotten Marie Konti in her soft warm arms.

I said, 'I caught the first plane back to Istanbul, leaving Berny to enjoy himself.' I went and opened the door into the corridor. 'Maybe you'd like to try finding your own rooms, brothers.'

They took their time about strolling

out. Tony paused to sniff at my hair, and then he made a clicking noise with his tongue in the manner of a vulgar G.I. and went out. I shut the door on them.

I went back and picked up that envelope and tore it open. Inside was a key, such as were used in this hotel. It had a brass check plate attached upon which was a room number. I held the key in my hand, and I thought, 'I wonder who sent me this invitation?'

Because only then at that moment did it occur to me that I might have made a mistake — that this might not be a pleasant invitation, but — a trap.

# 2

## I fall — off the bed

The fly walked into the spider's parlour. In other words, Joe P. Heggy went to find out who had given that invitation.

I went out into the corridor and I walked along it towards the elevator shaft. In my hand was this key that wasn't my own. The room number wasn't more than a dozen doors away from my own.

As I got to the door with the corresponding number I heard the elevator whine into life. That's an unusual sound in this hotel, because the damned thing's either out of order or else you can't find the old man who knows how to work the thing.

I inserted the key gently into that lock and quietly turned the key. I was just pushing the door open when I heard the elevator gate slam, and when I glanced that way I saw the old elevator man step out, and he was followed by a couple of men.

I didn't pay any attention to them, and I didn't give a damn if the elevator man saw me going into someone else's room. Joe P. Heggy is kind of uninhibited on occasions. This was an occasion.

I went inside, and quietly closed the door after me. Sometimes I take the precaution of slipping a bolt on a door, but I didn't on this occasion, because I thought I might have to get out quickly.

I was only backing a hunch, after all. I went across the tiny hallway and began to open the door that didn't lead into the bathroom. The door began to swing open of its own accord. I stood there and let it swing, so that I could see the room in its entirety.

For one second I thought the room was empty. Then someone moved.

It was a girl. She had been lying on the bed, and I knew she had been waiting for me.

It was the Rumanian who had sat next to me in the plane.

She was dressed, if you can call those

thin, summery garments dresses. And she began to rise up from the bed as I walked in.

I said, 'Don't you move on my account, honey.'

She went through the routine of trying to get up off the bed, but Joe P. Heggy was already sitting on it and smiling at her and holding her soft warm forearm. She couldn't get up after that, and she didn't try much.

She looked demure. A girl's got to look demure, caught under such circumstances. I looked down at her and saw the black, curving eyelashes that seemed to rest on those full-rounded cheeks of hers.

She was lying back on her elbows now, in a half-sitting position.

I drawled, 'Fancy finding you in this room.' As if I hadn't guessed.

She didn't pretend after that. She lifted those eyelashes and smiled at me with eyes that knew full well the value of a smile to a man. I looked more closely at her, and I saw those red lips were parted a little and there was the gleam of white teeth within.

I began to bend my head and she lifted her face very slightly and my lips brushed against her soft ones and I felt the warmth of her.

I came away so that I could look at her. She was worth kissing.

She went down on to the softness of that bed and her smile was inviting. I was in no hurry.

All the time I was looking down at her and I was wanting to know something. For that key through my door had been a bit sudden. But I didn't ask any questions; she could tell me when she wanted.

The sun's lingering afternoon rays just came in level through that window and it threw up the contours of her between myself and the window. She didn't say anything, but continued to look at me.

Then I began to get that old dryness in the mouth, the tightening at the back of the throat. My pulse began to rev up like a racing car engine on doped fuel.

My arms went round her and I held her so tightly it was probable she stopped breathing.

I got my lips against hers. She gave the slightest pretence of trying to push me away, and then abandoned the gesture towards maidenly modesty. Instead, I felt those soft, shapely arms wrap quickly round my neck.

We came up for air.

The girl said, 'There is something I must tell you.' She said it quickly, softly, and I saw a look of calculation in those lovely eyes.

I nodded agreeably. 'You go on and tell me, honey. I'll be here quite a while.'

She murmured, 'I have no money.'

With only half my mind, I said, 'So what? Who's got any money except the Aga Khan and Rita Hayworth? You've got your job, and that will pay your way for you.'

The luscious Rumanian whispered, 'I haven't a job. When I got here they told me that everything had fallen through.'

I wasn't listening to her, I thought I heard a sound, and it was nearer than it should have been. I looked over my shoulder, but the room was empty. I thought it would be one of those giant, scaly cockroaches that share Turkish hotel apartments with you.

I didn't mind how long the conversation lasted. Then I bent to kiss her again and her lips moved within an inch of my own, so that I could feel the warmth of her breath as she spoke. She was murmuring, 'It is serious. I cannot claim a breach of contract because the theatrical company who engaged me has gone bankrupt.' Her tongue peeped out and licked her lips as if she was coming to the critical part of her conversation. 'I would like to meet someone who would lend me money until I can find work.'

I let my lips come down on those soft ones again.

We were quiet for a few minutes and darkness was coming into that room now.

I came away, and said, 'Honey, you haven't got a worry in the world.'

And then I fell right off that bed.

I'd heard that sound again, and no mistake about it this time. Someone was in the room with me — and it wasn't just this Rumanian.

My head turned so quickly, I came

clean off that bed, and then I was up on my feet.

Two boys were standing just inside the room. The boys were around seventy-two inches each and topped two hundred pounds stripped.

They were dressed in natty suitings, more Turkish than the American style they aped, and they wore snap-brims pulled down level with eyes that were small and shining. For a second I didn't get that shine, thinking it was just interest in what they had been looking at.

They had big faces in the Turkish tradition. The kind of faces that look to have been stamped on a lot, and become flattened in the process, and are colour-lessly sallow.

I pulled my eyes round to that girl, because I wasn't sure this was a frame-up. I've had 'husbands' walk in on me before today and it's cost me plenty.

But one look at that girl and I knew she wasn't in on this. Her face was a mixture of indignation and fear.

I dragged my eyes away from her — and I mean dragged.

I turned to those big, silent bozos, watching me under the hat brims, and I said, 'You should knock. You might have caught me in an embarrassing situation.'

Then I stopped being the wisecracking alec.

One of the bozos had a gun in his hand.

It was a small, flat automatic, and the moment I saw it I knew this wasn't a case of someone coming mistakenly into someone else's apartment. Looking into those eyes I knew what they were after, too — me!

I stood for a moment, and I was suddenly remembering the whine of the elevator as I came into this room — remembering how two bozos had come out of the elevator just as I'd walked in on this Rumanian girl.

I was thinking that it would be natural for an elevator man to say, 'There's Mr. Heggy now, going into someone else's room.'

An exchange of small cash and the elevator man would probably find a key that opened up this apartment to Joe P.

Heggy's 'friends'.

I knew I'd got it all worked out, and it took me only a fraction of a second to do so. I hadn't lifted my hands, and they were dangling at my sides.

Only a sucker lifts his hands, as they do in the movies. When you've got your hands lifted above ear-level, you're a cooked duck — there's nothing much you can do.

But while your hands are down at your sides there's just a chance that you can use them . . .

I was thinking of one way how they could be used right now, but I hadn't the guts for it. The idea in my mind was just two centimetres short of suicide.

One of the bozos was pulling something out of his pocket. I was saying, 'What do you guys want with me?'

Because it was apparent it was me they were after by the way they ignored all that attractive feminine flesh sitting bolt upright on that bed.

Then I saw that second bozo come out with a knife. More, he came a couple of steps closer to me and he'd got that knife gripped in the ugliest manner possible — holding the haft so that the pointed blade came up beyond his thumb. You had a feeling that it was in a nice position to do an awful lot of damage, and I was just thinking, 'That's the way Habib Pasha was stabbed — by a knife that came into his heart from under his ribs.'

I got it right then that these boys were related to that political assassination, and it didn't make me feel any more comfortable. I started to think of that suicidal move with more favour.

The girl was swinging her legs off the bed. It was a curious gesture, that she should be concerned about her appearance with a man covering us with a revolver and another man padding forward with the obvious intention of using a knife on me.

I walked deliberately towards the man with the gun, but I was watching that other bub circling to get within range with his knife. Neither of the monkeys had spoken, but they seemed to be breathing hard and quickly, like men who are mentally prepared for a desperate thing. And all the time they were watching me from under their hat brims, their faces impassive, but their eyes like hooks trying to catch on to me.

So I did that suicidal thing. I put the safety-catch on that automatic, and that meant that the guy behind it couldn't trigger off a bullet into the Heggy body.

I did it quickly and neatly, just the way it's laid down in the book. It's what they teach G-men when they're going through the physical side of their training. It's called the last hope, and a man is advised to use the trick only when he knows that if he doesn't use it he's dead meat, anyway.

What you do is suddenly bring your hand up and knock back the barrel of the automatic. For that's the safety-catch on an automatic. Before you can fire one you've got to pull the barrel out.

If you slap the barrel it jumps back into the safety position automatically, and no amount of triggering will explode the round in the chamber.

That's just what I did. It sounds more difficult than in fact it turned out to be.

For that big monkey wasn't expecting anything so bold to happen to him. If I'd tried to grasp the automatic to wrest it from his grasp it would have given him that fraction of a second longer in which to trigger off a bullet in my direction. But that neat little action of shoving on to the barrel was so swiftly, so suddenly, done, that a very surprised Turk kept pulling on the trigger without realising that the gun had been made useless.

I was sweating from fear, as I'm told every G-man sweats when he tries out that trick at training school. But before the sweat got into my eyes I'd gone in at that monkey and slapped him so hard with a left and a right that be rocketed back against the wall and then fell on to a table and reduced it to pieces of wood.

He was out of the fight for a few seconds. But there was that other bozo with the ugly knife in his hand, and there was no safety-catch attached to that for me to shove back.

He was jumping in at me, his knife swinging, so I jumped in at him and I thought it would equalise matters if I kicked him on the jaw. I didn't get quite so high, but it must have hurt. His knife ripped a gash in my pants leg, and then he went back against the wall, coughing because his chest was suddenly red raw where I'd kicked him.

The girl started to scream. I don't blame her.

The first ape was coming off the wall, and he was trying to pull out the barrel of his gun now. I dived for him, and for a few seconds there was a whirl of arms and fists and feet. We socked each other and threw each other about and I never let that rube get more than a few inches away from me. In the end I threw him on to the floor with a thud that must have shaken the building, and then I stamped on his fingers and that got the gun out of his hand.

But I hadn't time to pick it up, because the boy with the knife was coming back, and he was snarling and saying things in Turkish that didn't need translation. That boy's mind was on his job now!

He was going to cut Joe P. Heggy into the smallest of pieces, and he was going to enjoy every bit of it.

I looked into that face, with its lips opened as he mouthed bad things about my future, and then I whirled away from the bozo on the floor and I knocked some of the teeth out of the knife boy's head.

I figured I was justified in doing what I was doing.

As he went back I went in with my knees, and every time they lifted they made that red-mouthed rube go sick and green.

There was a lot of noise from the corridor now, as somebody rattled on the door and then started to bang on it.

I turned, and I saw the boy who had held the automatic, but was no longer armed, roll over and then claw his way to the open window.

I didn't try to stop him. The boy with the knife still had the knife even though he was having difficulty in keeping his stomach down. I slapped him again, and sent him right across the room, and then I went jumping after him and I was saying things about his future that were on a par with what he'd told me about mine.

I kept hitting him all the way across the room and he kept trying to get that knife up at me but he was dazed and I was too quick every time.

He must have seen his buddy streaking out on to a fire escape, and he threw in the fight — he threw the knife at me, anyway, and while I was falling back to get out of its way, he went down that fire escape after his pal.

The Rumanian had stopped screaming, and she was looking at me and there was a lot of admiration in her eyes. Maybe Joe P. Heggy had been given a chance to acquit himself well in the eyes of a female.

I didn't go across to her, because there was blood on my hands, and there was rage in my heart. I went plunging across to the door and opened it and outside was a corridor full of guests and hotel servants. I looked out upon eager faces and flashing, excited brown eyes. I thought the best thing was for me to keep the girl out of it, and so I stepped into the corridor and shut the door after me. The girl could wait. She would wait I knew.

The manager was there, looking rounder

and more like an animated ball than ever. He shouted questions at me, wanting to know who had been murdered.

I shrugged and said some boys had bust into the lady's apartment. Maybe they'd been trying to steal things, I threw out, but I'd been visiting and had stopped them in their roguery.

It was the first story that came to my mind, but it satisfied the hotel proprietor. I didn't want to have more police attention. These things could drag on, especially if things came to court cases, and my job demands sudden moves and I didn't want to be tied down to Istanbul.

At the time I didn't realise how serious the whole situation was for me.

I started to go on to my room, thinking to put some plaster on my split knuckles, and then I saw big ginger, Marty Dooley come thumping up the staircase the elevator being once more out of action because the old man was interested in this schemozzle.

And Marty was so excited that I just stood and stared at him. He came fighting his way through the throng, shouting all the time at me. I began to gather what he was saying.

There was trouble out on the construction site. Plenty trouble. I was needed out there without loss of time.

Marty grabbed me by the arm and started to drag me down the stairs. I went, protesting. I'd just been in one fight and I wanted to get over that. What in hell's name was happening at the site, I kept demanding.

Marty shouted, 'There's a mob gathering out there. They're making speeches and turning ugly.'

And then he said savagely, 'Your blasted strong arm men aren't any good. They're listening to the speeches.'

I didn't get it.

We went down those stairs, and now I was going without assistance, because if there was trouble at the site it was my job to go out and attend to it. I'm the trouble-buster of the outfit, and I don't do any work until there's trouble demanding the personal and physical attention of Joe P. Heggy.

# 3

You still alive?

Down in the foyer Dwight Laite was just coming in from a back bar. Gorby Tuhlman was right behind him. Gorby is Gissenheim's boss engineer overseas. Evidently Dwight was rounding up all the boys he could find.

The foyer was quite crowded, because it was coming evening and that's when Istanbul wakes up. Everyone — hotel guests and staff — stood around and stared as the Americans came running into the foyer, nearly all of them bawling their heads off.

Dwight shouted, 'Hang on, we've got some grease monkeys in the back bar. I'll drag 'em out.'

I was beginning to get over that fight I'd just had, and I was still feeling pleased with myself. I mean, any guy feels good when he's just licked a couple of armed hoods in front of a girl he's with.

Another thing that made me feel good was that key in my pocket. I hadn't turned that in to the Rumanian girl yet. I thought, 'Next time I get near enough I'll ask her for her name.'

And then I thought, 'The next time I get near enough I won't bother about names.'

Marty told me all he knew. A 'phone call had come through from Harry Sauer, out at the site. People were streaming up from the town, and they were holding meetings on the edge of the excavations. The Turkish staff had quickly hold him what the meetings were about — this was the Ultra-Nationalist Party, and the orators were urging their supporters to go and sling the American imperialists and their equipment plumb into the middle of the Bosporus.

I said, 'The Ultra-Nationalist Party, huh?' That made me think a lot. 'They're using this Habib Pasha killing as an excuse to get at us — and they're sure moving fast!'

It made my brain go fast, too, because

somehow the tempo was too fast. I got a feeling then that that killing had triggered something off, and that the people back of the U.N.P. were having to do things in frantic haste.

The first was to remove me — only those two monkeys had been a mite slow and hadn't succeeded. Now the whole thing was being given a political aspect. They were using the opportunity to try to further their political objectives.

Marty said, 'You're in jake, anyway, Joe.'

The way he said it made me stare. 'I'm always in jake.'

'But not like this — not quite like this.' Marty jerked out a Camel and grinned at me as he flipped his lighter to it. He said, 'The paper that supports the U.N.P. has got special editions out on the street — and guess what they're saying in it?'

I made a couple of guesses, and then I threw in. 'You tell me.'

'They've named the killer of Habib Pasha.'

That made me blink, but I didn't say anything. I waited because I knew that Marty had a shock in store for me.

Marty looked disappointed because I didn't articulate, so he threw in the big surprise.

'The paper says it's obvious who the killer was. It was an American — '

I opened my mouth and then shut it quickly.

' — and the American was the man who first discovered the corpse. Only, *they* say, the American who said he discovered the corpse.'

I jerked out a cigarette then. 'Meaning. They've fixed the name of Heggy to the killing?'

Marty nodded, his green eyes gleaming happily under his light-coloured eyebrows. You'd have sworn Marty was enjoying the situation that I was in. He was — a whole lot. That's the kind of friends I have!

I drew in and expelled slowly through my nostrils. I was thinking hard. It wasn't good to feel that a murderer's label had been pinned on me, here in a city where so many were hostile to America.

I said, 'It's damned stupid. I was sixty feet up at least — '

'The paper doesn't say that. The paper says you rushed through the Customs because you'd seen Habib Pasha outside. They say you killed him, and there's witnesses who say they came running round the corner and saw you rising from the body with the knife sticking in its back.'

I said, cynically, 'It sounds so good they'll have me believing it soon.'

That wasn't important, but what could be important was the police reaction to this theory. After all, it added up just as plausibly as my story that I'd seen the man killed while I was coming in on an aircraft.

We were still waiting for those grease monkeys, when something big and soft got itself through the main doorway. I turned, seeing the expression on Marty's face. I saw a big, heavy American businessman complete down to the last detail of octagonal, rimless glasses. The picture of a prosperous and ruthless American tycoon, if you didn't know him.

The trouble was, we knew him. He was the boss — Berny Gissenheim himself.

And we knew him to be a craven louse of a man underneath that bluster of ruthless business efficiency. He didn't take us in any more.

We sneered at him openly as he came trundling across. We've got a theory that it does the boss good to show him our contempt now and then.

B.G. was red right round his fat neck, and his eyes were bright with rage as they looked on me. He started to bawl me out, right there in front of everyone, and I knew he was pretty agitated to make him do that. He should have learnt by now that Joe P. Heggy doesn't take kindly to a public bawling.

He shouted, 'Heggy, you're fired. You don't go 'plane riding without first asking my permission, see?'

I brightened at that. 'I'm fired? The hell, that's the best news I've heard in years. I'm going right back to bed, and they can do what they like out at the site.'

But Marty had grabbed me and was bawling the boss out now. 'You shut that big mouth of yours. Dammit, why don't you keep out of this business! Heggy's the trouble-buster, and right now there is a mountain of trouble wanting busting out at the site.'

That made Berny blanch. He went in mortal dread of losing some big contract and having to go and report it to that invalid but terrifying father of his back in Detroit.

He said, quickly, to me. 'I wasn't meaning it, Joe. You know I never mean it.' And then some of his indignation came back and his voice lifted so that everyone there could hear him. 'You shouldn't have run out on me like you did, that's all.'

I made my voice just as loud. So what, if he wanted everyone to hear, they could hear — and they'd hear my side of the story, too.

My eyes were on something small and frightened that was approaching our group.

I bawled, 'What are you talking about, B.G.? Didn't you run away from Istanbul? There wasn't any work for us to do in Athens, and you know it. You ran away from a woman!'

I let that remark sear in. I saw B.G. wince and look agitated and his hand fluttered in a signal to me to keep my mouth shut or at least keep my voice down.

I did neither. I said, 'When I found I was being taken to play nurse to you I came back. You're too big for a nurse now, B.G.'

That made him flush like a choirboy who has caught a girl's eye.

Marty came in then, Marty would. He loved taking the skin off the boss. He gave a big smile that was full of teeth and said, 'So you caught the next plane back when you found li'l Joseph had returned to Istanbul. You weren't scared of being in a strange, foreign city all by yourself, now, were you?'

We all knew the boss was terrified of foreigners, and in fact Joe P. Heggy was as much bodyguard-companion to him as trouble-buster for the firm.

B.G. was looking like a man who has started something and wishes to hell he hadn't. He teetered around, a big, fat hulk of a man who wasn't half as old as he tried to look. The other boys twitted him, and they knew they were safe, because the boss couldn't fire any of them. He'd made too many mistakes himself and they knew his weaknesses.

Tony Geratta put in some words then. 'You coming out to the site, B.G.?'

B.G. blinked. Then he asked, cautiously, 'What's the trouble?'

They told him. B.G. said, sure, he'd come out to the site. Only first he'd have a shower and change.

He made it sound hearty and even enthusiastic, but we knew better. The boss was running out on us. He wouldn't show up at the site until the trouble was over.

Then he saw that shrinking, timid creature. His face went white and then it went red, and then he started to move rapidly away from the centre of the lounge.

But Marty, Dwight, Gorby and Tony were standing like a wall right behind him now, and there were malicious grins on their faces. This was their idea of good fun — ribbing the boss. He wanted to retreat, and they knew why, so they stood in his way so that he couldn't get the hell out of it.

And all the time that timid little woman was approaching as if under some spell of fascination — like a rabbit that will come nearer the swaying head of a snake.

Only I couldn't make up my mind which one was the rabbit.

I said, 'Lav, honey, didn't you get a cable from B.G. asking you to go to Athens?'

B.G. looked horrified and then shot an accusing glance at me. He must have guessed then what I had done. But it was evident my plan had misfired, otherwise little Lav would have been in Athens now and not here in Istanbul.

I looked into that face that wasn't young and hadn't been young for ten years at least. And yet it had the lingering remains of prettiness about it. Her figure was like that, too. Your first thought was that she was a going-old spinster with no physical attractions, and then you notice that though she was small she was in good shape. That was what the boys had been saying lately, that little Lav had everything, after all.

She was looking at B.G. as she answered my question, and her eyelids were fluttering like a maiden looking on her first love. I heard her whisper, 'There wasn't a seat on the Athens aircraft today.'

I thought cynically, 'That's the way it is!'

You work out a nice little scheme and then the thing goes bust because you have overlooked a final possibility — the fact, for instance, that an aircraft might be full. But as things had turned out, it was just as well little Lav hadn't wasted her money going to Athens.

The light of her life had come back to her.

They were still waiting for the rest of the boys to turn up, and Dwight was getting agitated and bawling to people to come running up. He'd got transport all ready outside the hotel door. But the boys wouldn't miss this chance to take the shine off their boss.

Wickedly they made him feel as uncomfortable as possible.

Tony Geratta got in front of blushing little Miss Dunkley, the frustrated English woman, and he wagged his finger and said, 'Don't you get to ruining little Berny while we're away. Berny's a good boy, and if ever there's been a boy scout in man's pants it's B.G. Leave him alone, get me?'

Lavinia looked so embarrassed it was nearly pitiful. Nearly — but not quite, because she didn't run away even then. Back in Lavinia's little mind was one all-powerful obsession, and that was to get a man and make up for all she had missed in her restricted English life to date. The pity was she had picked on a sap like B.G.

B.G. came shoving his stomach forward, and he was yapping his head off, telling Tony he ought to be ashamed of himself for speaking the way he did. Tony just grinned.

Then the grease monkeys came into the foyer, and at that the party went running out to get the transport. I went with them.

The last I saw was big B.G. standing uneasily in the middle of that hotel foyer, looking at the little Englishwoman in a manner so doubtful it was nearly comical. And little Miss Dunkley was taking a timid step nearer him — timid, and yet it didn't hesitate.

Lavinia had her hooks in this man and he wasn't going to get away from her.

That was the last I saw. I got into the truck and I was thinking that I'd rather have stayed around the hotel where that Rumanian dish was,

We went out as fast as our Turkish driver could take us, and it was coming dusk and so we needed headlights. Some of the boys didn't know what it was all about, so Dwight and Marty told them.

They were pretty smart at my expense.

'The strong-arm boys that Joe P. Heggy booked to guard the equipment don't seem to have done anything except throw in with the agitators,' Dwight said sarcastically. 'The hell, what's the good of paying these boys if they go on to the other side just when we need them!'

I didn't say anything. In these countries this sort of thing wasn't unusual. You pay watchmen, and when there was any trouble you couldn't find the watchmen for dust. I'd tried to be a bit smarter, here in Istanbul, and I'd engaged a bunch of the strongest men in Asia.

They were the porters — those men of fantastic strength, who carry enormous loads on their backs and are to be seen everywhere in Turkey and other Eastern countries today, in spite of the competition of the internal combustion engine.

I let Dwight go on. I was fingering that key and thinking of a lost moment. It was maddening to think that those two uglies had walked in when they had. Now if they'd fixed to arrive ten minutes later . . .

Suddenly we came out above the site Gissenheim's had been brought in with their dirt-shifting equipment to move a hill that spoilt a runway long enough to take the latest in atom bombers. There was a lot of feeling in Istanbul because an American firm had got the contract in the face of local tenders,

But the trouble was that the local contractors hadn't the equipment of the American companies, and it would have taken too long to move that hill by hand. In any event, Uncle Sam reckoned that as he was paying the bills the thing was to get the job done properly and Gissenheim's had been given the contract.

There'd been sabotage attempts before, but never anything like this that my eyes fell upon now.

The equipment was all centred where that hill was sliced in half by the mighty muck-shifters. We could see a towering grab, and smaller cranes and long conveyer belts leading to giant hoppers. There was a concentration of grubbers and bulldozers and long-armed diggers. There was almost a village of this equipment and the maintenance huts that had been erected to service them.

Just now the big floods were on and the white glare lit up the scene. It looked for a moment as if the equipment park was besieged by an army.

Our driver, though a Turk himself, simply stood on the accelerator and drove us through that yelling mob right up to where Harry Sauer was standing on top of a bulldozer trying to talk to them. He didn't seem to be meeting with much success, but probably his intention was just to play for time until the rest of the Gissenheim executives got out to him.

He looked a very relieved man when he saw us, because Harry was only assistant engineer. Responsibility now passed onto others' shoulders.

Marty took the lead. He swung out of the car and ran over to Harry. There must have been several hundred Turks in that crowd, and most of them looked young, as though they were students. That's usually what you find — that extreme Nationalism is stronger among the student classes than anywhere else.

They had crude-lettered placards and banners up, and everyone was shouting at once and urging everyone else on to do something. When they saw us pour out of that big transport the crowd came forward with a rush.

I heard Harry shout, 'They are talking about bustin' up everything. They like to talk, or they'd have done it a long time back, too.'

But evidently even they had got tired of talk and now we could see they meant action.

There was an ugly rush, and we Americans found ourselves being forced back against the bulldozer upon which Harry was standing. We didn't fight at first, but let ourselves go back, but when we began to feel hurt we lashed out and did quite a bit of damage.

It wasn't a promising situation, however. I yelled, 'This is a job for the cops!'

Harry shouted back, 'I sent for them half an hour ago.'

That, I thought, was just like the cops. They never got anywhere. Then a big ugly who wasn't so well-dressed and wasn't so young as most of that crowd, came lurching through and tried to take my head off with a swinging fist. I went down a little, so that the blow travelled past me. Then I came in under that extended arm and tried to cave in his chest with a snapping right hook. He went back hurt.

I realised there were two others where he had been, and they weren't so well-dressed and weren't students, either. They came jumping in at me, and I saw a knife.

I got an idea then. The idea that these

three rubes were singling me out for special treatment under cover of this ruckus. I thought: They're trying to do what those two rubes failed to do back at the hotel.

Somehow I got away from the man with the knife by falling back among the fighting crowd. They were all fighting now.

We never like to start a shindig with citizens of these lands wherein we work, but when someone takes a poke at you, you are inclined to take a poke back.

But we couldn't hold off this yelling mob that pressed on us in a wild flurry of fists and feet. They meant business. They were going to lynch these Americans and bust up their equipment for them.

Turkey for the Turks! That was the cry they were yelling. They regarded our presence there as an act of enslavement to the Almighty Dollar. Mebbe there was some truth in it at that.

Harry got the bulldozer going and started to chum around among the crowd. He didn't do any damage with it and that wasn't the intention, but for a few moments it kept them back and that gave us a breathing space.

Marty roared, 'Gorby, get up and operate that grab!'

Gorby tumbled to the idea at once. It was a trick we'd employed with labour troubles before.

Gorby went running across among the huts until he came to the giant grab. He went climbing up the long steel ladder to where the cabin perched in the sky and we heard him start the engine,

We were fighting again, keeping close together and trying not to get encircled. Harry kept brushing the opposition away from us like flies with his bulldozer, but some of the young Turks had started to jump onto the tractor and were trying to pull Harry away from the controls. We rushed in and pulled them off, and Harry kept up the work a little longer.

We saw a hut go up in flames and knew that more of the U.N.P. had gone over to acts of destruction. We saw others going into the other tool sheds and there was the sound of breaking metal.

It filled us with fury. We hadn't

recovered from previous acts of sabotage, and our spares were precious. We went lashing about, trying to stop the young fools, but we didn't get anywhere with it. All we got was a thrashing.

Some of the boys were looking very bloody now, and were staggering, and the crowd had got the lust for blood in their minds and were coming in, trying to finish us off brutally. Then Gorby came in and stopped their nonsense.

He'd got the giant grab scuttling down among the loose earth and now he swung the grab right over where the U.N.P. supporters were at their most crowded. He just opened the grab and tons of muck came whooshing down upon the Turks.

Immediately Gorby swung the grab and got another bite of dirt, only this time the Turks were watching that grab and when I came swinging over them they scattered and ran for it.

It's no fun having a few tons of even dry, light soil showered over you.

There's always something comical about a mob when it gets on the run. And mobs are quick to panic. They started to run away from that giant grab which came chuntering forward on its caterpillar tracks, that mighty arm manoeuvring with incredible rapidity to bring tons of earth on the heads of the agitators.

I got an impression of men trying to get out of the way of that muck, while still trying to get back and do damage to the Gissenheim equipment . . . and the Gissenheim executives.

There was a bedlam of sound, as engines roared, and everyone was shouting, and the whole scene looked fantastic under those lights that were strung up, all around the equipment park I saw car headlights swinging across the rough ground a mile or so to the east. But I didn't have long to watch the scene.

Those same bozos were back at me. They weren't interested in anyone else or in smashing Gissenheim equipment.

Plainly all they wanted was to smash up Joe P. Heggy.

I'd gone back against the wall of a toolshed when I realised that I was on the spot, and I wouldn't move away from it, because that would have given my enemies a chance to jump me from the rear. I saw the bozos come lurching out from the crowd, heading straight for me.

There was a brief whirl of violent activity, in which I felt justified again in using my feet. It was a case of my feet against knives, anyway.

I got ripped down the sleeve of my coat, and I know blood came, but it didn't damage a muscle. I crashed in at them, hurling myself unexpectedly away from the wall. I saw a heavy face with dull, small eyes that were drowned in pools of shadow in the floodlights. I started to knock his face right round to the back of his head, and he couldn't stand the punishment and went down. Then I went back against the wall, hearing the sounds of fighting all around me, and being conscious of the occasional blinding flash of light from those car headlights.

The other two came swinging in again at me, and I kicked out and kept them beyond arm's reach. The sweat was pouring from my face. It was one of those close, still nights that you get in Istanbul in summer.

My clothes were sticking to my back and to my limbs, and seemed to restrict my movements.

But when those bozos came lurching back to finish me off, I found myself agile enough. I started to run alongside that wall, and that brought them wheeling after me. Suddenly I turned and crashed back in among them, again taking them by surprise at the unexpectedness of my assault. One bozo went down and I think I'd broken his nose. There was a lot of blood and he was sobbing.

I didn't feel any sorrow for him because even then he was still holding that knife and hadn't lost the intention of carving me,

I went down on one knee, and I saw those two bozos swinging down with their knife arms. They were very clearly revealed, and that must have meant the arrival of those cars.

I fell back, scrambling desperately to keep out of reach of those knife blades.

And then big, uniformed figures were

at those two boys, smacking them up against the wall.

I got the sweat out of my eyes and realised that the cops had come. They were holding two of my assailants against that wall, but the third man, the one with the broken smeller, seemed to have disappeared.

I don't like Turkish police, generally. They are big, brutish looking men, though maybe that's because they wear a uniform modelled on the German S.S. style.

But I was mighty glad to see them then. I stood and panted and watched a couple of dozen cops rush at that crowd and send them flying like rabbits into the darkness beyond the equipment park. But the U.N.P. didn't go away at that. They gathered together in the darkness and got their courage back and began to shout threateningly at the police as well as the Gissenheim crowd.

Then I saw a man — a civilian — get out of a car and go and walk towards where the milling mob could just be seen on the edge of the lighted area. He held up his hands and in the distance I could hear his voice talking to that crowd.

A big young cop came across to me. He was an officer, and seemed in charge of this army of police. I recognised him. He was my friend from Istanbul — the one the boys sometimes called George.

The police officer had a smile on his face when he saw me. Quite cheerfully he said, in his very good English, 'What, are you still alive?'

I said, 'Just.'

The smile seemed to leave his face then. I heard him say, 'You'd better watch out. I don't think you're going to live much longer.'

I shared his opinion. Plainly there were people after me who meant murder. I nodded towards that civilian, talking to the crowd. I said, 'Who's the orator?'

The police officer said, 'That's Mustapha Agloul. He's the new head of the U.N.P. since Habib Pasha went out.'

He looked at me, and then called out, 'Where are you going?' Because I started to walk towards that man, haranguing his supporters.

I didn't say anything. But I was

remembering what Tony Geratta had said back in the hotel. That perhaps some political aspirant within the U.N.P. might have bumped off Habib Pasha for promotion purposes. I wanted to take a glimpse at Mustapha's face, because I thought it might be the one I'd seen under that hat the moment the knife slid under Habib's ribs.

George put a big hand on my shoulder and I stopped walking. He said. 'I don't know what's in your mind, but you won't live if you get near to that mob. They're convinced that Joe P. Heggy did in fact kill their leader, and they'd like to even scores.'

I looked sourly at Mustapha Agloul. I said, 'I've got an idea the killer might be right over their now.'

George probably knew what I meant. These police officers know the depth of the intrigues of politicians of all parties.

But he said, 'I can't let you go over. Mustapha Agloul came to talk his supporters out of violent action. That's what he's doing now.'

I sneered. 'Yeah, he's telling 'em to be

good boys. I'll bet a grand only an hour ago he was pep-talking 'em into comin' out here to bust up Gissenheim's.'

The police officer didn't say anything, not about Mustapha. Instead he spoke about my health.

'Mr. Heggy, you don't seem to realise that you are now a man with a few million enemies. The whole U.N.P.'s got it in for you, and if you take my advice you'll get out of this country. There's no safety for you now in Turkey, not with this suspicion against you. As a police officer I must inform you that we cannot take responsibility for your safety.'

It made me blink. Have you ever thought of having a few million enemies, many of them hating you so much they'd feel glad to do you in? I didn't feel very happy, and that is the greatest understatement of my life. In fact I felt — horrified.

George looked at me like a man who is friendly and he said, 'I'll give you police protection and you can go away on the night plane.'

I said, 'I'm scared to death. I've never been so scared in my life.' And then I said, 'But I'm not running away.'

There was blood pumping up into my brain now, and it was hot, raging blood. I hadn't killed Habib Pasha and I wasn't going to run away like a frightened criminal. Just at that moment I was remembering I was a trouble-buster — that I went out and bust up trouble, and didn't run away from it.

The hell, I was saying to myself, I don't leave this city until the name of Heggy is cleared!

It was a hotheaded, angry sentiment, but right then I was a hotheaded, angry man.

George grinned. I think he'd expected something like that from me. He shrugged and said, 'Don't say I didn't tell you. From now on you'll not be able to move anywhere in this city without someone coming up to stick a knife in your back. I can't give you a police escort, because my instructions are to offer you protection until you get on a plane leaving this country. If you stay here, you stay at your own risk and you're on your own.'

I said, bad-temperedly, 'I'm on my own.'

I walked away. Mustapha Agloul seemed to have settled his crowd. They'd started to stream away towards the city, and it looked as though we were all right for the rest of the night. The police officer said he'd leave half a dozen men to make sure the U.N.P. didn't return with any violent intentions; and then, at that moment, some of our watchdogs came padding forward out of the gloom.

They were the men I'd recruited to be guards over the equipment park. They were the porters, the strong men of Istanbul, who could carry a house on their shoulders, almost. I'd figured that they were just the boys for standing up against saboteurs, but it seemed they weren't a damned bit of good.

I went over to speak to them. There were a dozen of them, about. They weren't very tall men, but they were so broad it was incredible, and the muscles on their limbs and bodies were like lumps of ridged concrete.

They stood sheepishly before me, and

they were barefooted, with old, torn and soiled shirts on their mighty backs, and pants in rags around their massive lower limbs. They watched me from under matted hair, so that they looked like primitive Early Men.

I remembered, the first time I'd seen them in their underground dwelling, I'd thought them troglodytes.

I went up to them and I cussed them plenty. They didn't understand a word I said. I told them they were fired, and they just looked at me and didn't understand. Then they must have got tired of my voice, and they all drifted away to the watchman's hut where they began to cook coffee in those tiny copper Turkish coffee pots.

It made me hopping mad. But there wasn't anyone there at the moment who could speak Turkish, so I turned away, figuring they were still on the payroll.

The boys were coming in, now. I hadn't realised there was so many American employees on this airfield project. Something like twenty executives were out there that night, and in fact the only absentee seemed to be the boss himself, B.G.

Some of the boys weren't feeling so good because they'd taken a beating, and these were shoved into cars and taken off to hospital. But most of the men were all right and were examining the equipment to see what damage had been done. Marty came over to me and said, 'They've done a lot of damage to the tool shop. Gorby's going crazy.'

I said, 'I know Gorby. He'll be all right tomorrow.' And knowing Gorby, I figured he'd patch up the broken equipment so that Gissenheim's could keep going. The police had arrived just in time to stop any serious sabotage.

Dwight, Marty, Tony and some of the others had grouped round me and the police officer. George looked at Marty very levelly and said, 'You won't know Mr. Heggy long. He doesn't know what's healthy for him.'

The boys looked as if they weren't very bothered if something did happen to me,

So the police officer was saying again, 'There's a strong rumour among the

U.N.P. that Mr. Heggy bumped off their leader. A few million people don't like him any more, and they'll try to do him in — at least, some of them will. I've offered Mr. Heggy an escort to the plane to get him out of the country, but he says he's staying here.'

Marty looked at me under those ginger eyebrows of his. His eyes looked contemptuously at me and I glowered. He said, 'He's got a skull thicker than most. It'll take some time for the truth to penetrate. Maybe he'll be dead by the time it does.' And there was a hopeful note in his voice as if that was quite an interesting possibility.

I said, 'I don't run out like that chicken-livered boss of mine would. I'm staying, and I don't leave Istanbul until we find the murderer of Habib Pasha.'

I was thinking I'd like to see Mustapha Agloul. If I could identify him . . .

Everybody looked kindly at me, in the way they look at people about to die. It kept my temper boiling hotter than ever.

Tony said, 'Where are you going to hide in Istanbul, sap?'

I said, darkly, 'I know a place or two.'

The police officer said brusquely, 'Then I'd get to one of those places quickly. I'm leaving you now. I hope you're alive in the morning.'

He walked away, big and very smart in his uniform and looking the picture of efficiency. He went like a man who washes his hands of an unpleasant situation.

Marty got me by the arm and started to push me across to a car. He said, 'You're an unhealthy subject to be around this place. As a trouble-buster you're a wash out. Until the real murderer's found you're useless on the job. So — keep the hell away from the site.'

I was inclined to argue because I was in that frame of mind. But then I realised that Marty was right. I could only bring more trouble on the site. The thing for me to do was to go into hiding until the police discovered the murderer. I had ideas on that subject, however, and I thought maybe I'd be able to discover something of the truth myself.

I went across to that car and Marty and

Dwight came with me. They were sarcastic at my expense, but I knew they were concerned about me. They just weren't the kind of men to get sentimental. We got into the car and started to bump long the dirt road that led on to what passes around Istanbul for a first-class highway. As we were travelling through the night, seeing only a path ahead cleft into the darkness by our headlights, Dwight, who was driving, asked, 'Where do you figure on hiding?'

I said, 'A place I know downtown. It's one place the U.N.P. won't think of searching.' Then I remembered something. I said, 'I've got to call at my apartment first to pick up something.'

Dwight flashed his teeth in a pleasant smile. 'Yeah? You wouldn't be thinking of dropping in on that nice Rumanian woman that you've been talking about?'

I said, 'I haven't been talking about her. I figure someone else must have been doing the talking.'

Then Marty and Dwight fell to arguing, and the upshot of it was they decided it wasn't good for me to go back into that hotel. It was arranged that Marty would go up to my room and get the parcel I'd mentioned. They didn't know it, but it was a parcel of nylon stockings. If they'd known, it would have made them wonder.

We came driving down that highway, and suddenly we ran right into a mob of men hurrying back to the city. They were the U.N.P. supporters, returning home. We had to crawl to pass through them, and the boys made me get down out of sight. Even so the crowd got a bit anti-American when they recognised the occupants of the car, and they tried to stop it and turn it over.

But Dwight kept his foot on the accelerator, shoving his way through the crowd at a steady ten miles an hour. A couple of windows were smashed and for a few moments it seemed a pretty ugly situation, but then Dwight got the car through and we could forget about the incident.

It just altered the plans a little.

Marty had stopped some glass with his cheek and there was quite a nasty wound and the blood was making a mess of things. The wound wasn't serious, and could be patched up quickly. But Marty didn't want to stay in a shirt and suit that was warm and sticky with blood.

So Marty went with Dwight into the hotel — Marty to get attention, and Dwight to fetch that parcel for me.

They parked the car in a side alley, where they were sure it wouldn't be recognised. I was told to stay where I was, and I sat and glowered in the darkness and fumbled for a cigarette. I didn't like a passive role.

But I recognised it was all for the best. I'd got ideas simmering at the back of my mind, and it suited me to get away from this dangerous hotel for the night.

The only thing was that being so near I couldn't help thinking of that cabaret-burlesque artist. She was worth thinking about and I couldn't get out of my mind that picture of her when I came falling off that bed.

I sat back in the darkened interior of that car and I smoked a couple of quick cigarettes. In spite of what the boys had said the urge was coming stronger every moment for me to duck out of the car and spend an hour at least with that Rumanian. I knew she'd like me to.

But I didn't, though. I thought I'd do as the boys said and I'd leave the Rumanian dish for another night.

I was just meditating when the door jerked open violently and something mountain-sized lurched into the car.

# 4

## Nylons for Baby

I started to swing. The action was instinctive. All I saw for that first moment was a big, hulking shadow, and I knew it was neither Dwight nor Marty.

Then I caught a flash of light reflecting on rimless glasses and my fist pulled back just in time.

Something big and soft and quivering sank down on to the seat by my side. I relaxed back in my corner and drew upon my cigarette.

I said, 'What are you doing out so late at night, B.G.?' For this was the boss.

He said, quickly, 'I saw Dwight. He told me, you were down here. I came in a hurry.'

I told him, 'I could see you were in a hurry. What's biting you?'

I could hear him lick his lips in the darkness, and though I couldn't see his face, I knew it was palpitating with fear. I made a guess as to the cause of this fear, too, and it turned out to be right.

He almost moaned, 'It's that woman.'

'Lav?'

'Lav.' I saw his big, fat head nod. 'My God. She hasn't left me alone a minute since I got back to the hotel.'

He leaned across towards me and I saw the expression on his face and it was filled with incredulous disbelief.

He almost whispered, 'You wouldn't know the things she tried to do. She even got into my room. You know I don't like that way of going on.'

I said. 'You amaze me.'

He got nasty with me then and started to say that all men weren't built alike. 'Now, you, Heggy, you think it's good fun to lead a woman on. But I don't. You know I'm — '

I flipped a sarcastic paw. 'Don't tell me. You're Saving Yourself Up For The Right Woman When She Comes Along. Me, I don't understand it. I'm still waiting for the right woman, but I enjoy myself meantime.'

He said, 'You don't seem to understand. She's trying — ' He gulped. ' — trying
to seduce me.' I could feel him quivering
in fat indignation at the thought.

I said, cynically: 'Okay, boss, but what
is there I can do about it?' If he thought
I was going to take Lavinia off his hands
he was mistaken.

All he could say was, 'What can I do?'

I told him, briefly and tersely, and he
looked shocked.

He said, 'I won't do it! That's the last
thing I want to happen.'

I shrugged. I couldn't think of anything
else.

Berny said, 'You're my trouble-buster — '

'Not this kind of trouble,' I said bluntly.

B.G. was so agitated he even tried
shaking my arm. He yapped, 'I'm not
staying in this hotel without you around,
Joe. If you're going into hiding, so am I,'

He was only the boss, so I told him he
could go sit on his face. He wasn't
coming with me. The plan I had in mind
didn't embrace the fat-bottomed Berny
Gissenheim, and I told him so.

He fired me again, a couple of times in

quick succession. That didn't worry me. Then Dwight came back with that parcel and I shoved Berny out into the alley. Dwight told him to go chase himself for a couple of hours, and that got B.G. mad. He always got mad when his employees talked to him like that, but there wasn't much he could do about it.

They were good employees, and they knew too much about B.G. and his terror of the old man in the bath chair back in Detroit.

Dwight pulled the car out on to the main street of Pera. As he came nosing through the pedestrian traffic that thronged the sidewalk at that time of night, he called back to me, 'Where now, killer's meat?'

I winced. I didn't like to think of myself as meat. I swallowed and said, 'Get me down across Galata Bridge.'

He sent the big automobile crashing along the stone-set road that dropped down to the wide iron bridge across the Golden Horn. When we were in the darkness of the commercial sector of Istanbul he pulled up alongside a big, gloomy warehouse building. I got out.

Dwight leaned anxiously across to speak to me through the open window, and I could see his face and there was genuine concern in it. The boys took their hell out of me, but I reckoned they had a soft spot for Joe P. Heggy at the bottom of it all.

He said, quickly, 'I don't like you going off on your own like this.'

I said, 'I don't like it myself. I know a place where I'll get a nice warm bed tonight, and I'll be welcome. I'm still in a mind to try it.'

Dwight said, 'You'd be dead meat if you did. You bet your life they're watching that dame's apartment.'

'Then,' I said, 'I'm better off down here. I wouldn't be safe in any other hotel in Istanbul, you can bet.'

I didn't feel that I'd be particularly safe down here — for here could be regarded as in the heart of the enemy territory. But I was relying on that. I was gambling boldly, and I figured this was one place they would never look for me.

Dwight looked uneasy, and then he

shrugged as much as to say, 'Well, it's your funeral.'

I gave a flip of my paw and started to walk away in the shadows of those high, gloomy buildings. Dwight pulled the car round and went back to the hotel.

I knew where I was going. I'd been there before. I walked with that parcel under my arm, and I thought: This is a life-saver.

I figured those nylons could do the trick if anything could. For nylons are now international currency, and, more than that, can find a way into any woman's heart. That was what I was depending on.

I walked down an alley that was full of sinister shadows. There weren't many people about, and in that near-darkness they wouldn't recognise me for a foreigner. I just kept walking close to the walls of those many office and warehouse buildings, and descended down to the water's edge.

The moon was up and beginning to ride high over to my left. I saw its brightness as I walked out from the end of the alley on to a rocky shore that gave down to the Golden Horn.

The moon shone on the gaunt black buildings of the business quarter of Istanbul, and made a long, gleaming bright ladder of light on the rippling waves of this fabulous harbour. It was a picture for the poetic. But I'm no poet.

I began to go down that rocky shore, and even as I descended I knew that eyes had seen me. Eyes always saw whoever came this way. I knew it from a past experience.

I didn't turn, but found a path along the rock-strewn shore and walked to where a great solid wharf reared stilt-legged on barnacled timbers out of the smelly waters. The wharf gave on to a long, low building, which I knew to be a chemical factory.

Joe P. Heggy had been here before.

I followed the path under the wharf, and now I was in almost complete darkness, but I could see a light reflecting on the water distantly, where the timbers stood out of the gently lapping estuary. But the light scarcely reflected at all at the back of the wharf, and I followed that path with difficulty.

But I knew which way to go, and if I lost the path at times I didn't lose my way. It was eerie work, because those massive supports seemed to stand closely round me, and there was something threatening in their shadowy appearance.

I kept thinking that enemies lurked behind them, and any moment they would come stepping out. Almost I could feel they were those boys who had tried to knife me. Then I remembered that two of them right now would be telling lies in an Istanbul jail.

I walked on and pretended I wasn't afraid. I don't mind facing two-legged danger, but I don't like things that give me the creeps.

I found what I was after. My hand fell against a curtain of rough hessian that seemed to spread across the rough rock wall that reared behind the wharf. I dragged it aside.

All I saw was a black hole in the wall of rock. I stood there, risking a lot, and nothing happened. So after a few seconds

I walked inside with my hands outstretched.

I could smell wood smoke, but it was old and I knew that no fire smouldered. I walked forward, confident that I wouldn't trip over anything, and after a few paces my hand met the rough-hewn rear wall.

Then I turned. I leaned against that wall and I waited.

I think I waited ten minutes before I heard a sound outside. But in all that time I had no doubts that my hunch had been right — that eyes had watched me come out of that alley and follow the path under the piles of the wharf.

I stood where I was because here in the blackness the entrance to this rock cave seemed like a lighted window. I could see the moonlight in the distance, dappling the wave broken surface of the estuary.

Suddenly I saw a movement outside. I saw something immense glide from the shadows and stand there in the moonlight. I sighed when I saw that mighty figure.

It was a girl, and I knew her. Once before I had met her and she had helped me and now I was bringing nylons to repay her for what she had done for me. She was one of the womenfolk of these porter people — a girl of uncertain age, perhaps sixteen, perhaps over twenty. And she was built like a tree herself; in her was all the strength of those mighty men from whom she sprang.

She was barefooted now as always, and I could see those great lusty limbs silhouetted against the moon-lit background. I could see shoulders wider than those on many a man. She was magnificent, but there was a bit too much of her for Joe P. Heggy. Mating with an elephant seemed just as reasonable.

I saw her peering suspiciously into the darkness and I gently pulled a nylon stocking out of that parcel and held it dangling in my band. She couldn't see it, and perhaps she wasn't sure I was inside that chamber — this little cave in which her menfolk often lived because all their labours weren't sufficient at times to rent a roof for them.

I could see the coarse hair that came over her face, making her almost as animal as her menfolk. And yet I knew she had quite a good face — broad across the cheekbones and browned by work in the sun. With laughing, almond eyes, and lips that opened in a great hearty grin that showed teeth so white and so big and so even, they would have been the envy of a Hollywood film actress.

She came advancing slowly into that chamber, and now I could see that that ragged dress of hers was more ragged than ever. This night there was a great rent in it.

She came in and I could hear her deep, rather quick breathing.

Because she had her back to the light she couldn't see a thing in that rocky chamber, and I had the advantage of her there. I reached out and let that nylon stocking float on to her strong bare neck.

She seemed to fall away at the touch, and I heard a little gasp that was almost fear — though what an Amazon like her had to fear I wouldn't know.

Then her hand found that stocking and in a second understanding had come to her. I heard the crooning cry of pleasure that is international — that comes to the lips of any woman who finds her fingers touching nylon.

I heard the Turkish girl whispering ecstatically, 'Nylon! Nylon!' That was the only English she spoke.

I stepped forward then into the moonlight, grinning. She saw me. She'd known I was there, of course, and she'd followed because she'd guessed what that parcel contained under my arm. I had promised her those nylons a few days back, and she'd known that Joe P. Heggy wouldn't go back on his word.

We both moved out of the rocky chamber, and now, by contrast, under the wharf seemed astonishingly bright.

It was a curious situation. For Turkish girls don't usually let themselves be found alone with strange males. The yashmak may have been abolished by Kemal Ataturk, but they still guard their womenfolk jealously.

She was scared of me, or at any rate scared of being found alone with me, but those nylons kept her from running away.

She pushed back her black hair so that

she could see that parcel the better, and her rather small, bright, brown eyes never left it for a second.

I wanted to make the most of what I'd brought, and I didn't just hand her the parcel. I shoved my hand in and brought out some packaged nylons, and I handed packet after packet across to her, prolonging the ecstasy as long as I could.

By the time she'd got her arms full she was almost delirious. Never in her life had this poor Turkish girl thought she could acquire such wonderful wealth.

Now she hadn't a thought in her head of her menfolk and any danger, and she didn't try to run away from me when she'd got the last of my nylons. Instead she couldn't wait. She flopped down on the stump of an old wharf pile and she opened one of those packages and with loving fingers carefully pulled those stockings on to her mighty limbs. I stood and looked down on her and grinned appreciatively.

When she'd got 'em on she stood up, and she didn't know how comical she looked in her tattered dress, with those shimmering aids to Western elegance on her trunk-like legs. And she had no shoes on, anyway.

But it does things to women to feel nylons upon their flesh and this girl was no exception. She was all soft inside, I reckon, because of the gift I had brought her.

After all, there aren't many girls anywhere who suddenly acquire fifty pairs of nylons,

I'd been rehearsing a little Turkish that I'd memorised from a Turkish-English dictionary I'd bought a few days back, and I was about to speak my piece when that mighty gal reacted unexpectedly.

I tell you, nylons do things to girls. Maybe the moon was helping, and the seeming safety of that quiet place under the wharf. And maybe she was like little Lavinia.

I stopped grinning, in sudden alarm as I saw the expression on that girl's moonlit face. She was looking brighter about the eyes — they were so bright you could have sworn she'd suddenly become drunk or had had a shot of dope in her arm.

I knew what sort of dope she'd had and I knew the dope she was looking at.

She seemed to stumble forward in those nylons, and one of them had sagged below her knee and the other was dropping. It made her look — exciting.

She came right up to me where I stood with my back against that wall into which had been dug the rocky chamber. I couldn't get away from her, and I don't think suddenly I wanted to get away. Yet I'd never thought of her that way.

She was all over me. She was making funny little noises in Turkish, and I knew what they added up to, because I had heard them in many a language.

I felt her ardent young body seeming to reach out and envelop me. And all the time I could feel her strength as she clasped me.

I looked into a face that was very close to mine. A face that was more Oriental than Occidental, a face I knew to be brown in daylight, but was white in this reflected moonlight. And her eyes seemed very large now, though normally they were rather small and faintly slit-eyed.

She wanted to reward me for what I had brought for her.

I got her and pulled her out of the moonlight, and I wasn't quite serious until we were in that complete black darkness. Then instinct was all there, and I was doing those things I hadn't thought of when I came along that path.

We were standing there when a shadow fell across the entrance.

That girl came away from me so fast it was fantastic. One moment she had been so ardent that it seemed nothing would stop her. Then that shadow fell across her, and the terrors of a lifetime of sex-segregation fell upon her.

I wasn't much behind her, because these Turkish menfolk do primitive things to males whom they catch with their sweethearts and daughters.

We crouched together, and I could feel the warmth of her bare arm against mine. Right in the entrance was a sinister figure. It was a man, but there was more gorilla about him than man. He was big enough for any two men, and he had the long arms of his kind — he was one of the porter breed, these men who can carry a grand piano on their backs — and do.

I could see him in his fluttering rags and knew him to be bare-footed, and I could sense, though I didn't see it, that he had the scrub face of his kind, and the small eyes almost lost under the shaggy protruding brows.

He began to come slowly, suspiciously into that cave. I heard the girl at my side whimper and I knew that she felt as if death was advancing on her. She touched my arm in the darkness. It wasn't a grip; it was too timid for that.

She just seemed to touch with her fingertips and then draw away from me, and yet I could feel what was in her mind.

In effect she was saying that I was all she could rely on. I didn't feel it was much to rely on right then. Joe P. Heggy's a big man in America and a strong man anywhere, but my strength is ordinary and these professional weightlifters are in the superman class.

But this girl looked to Joe P. Heggy to save her. I guessed right then that if that gorilla caught us both together, apart from what he'd do himself, there'd be something mighty unpleasant happen to Baby when the news got round. They tell me that the primitive Turkish male will do away with any female whom he thinks has betrayed his kind.

That was in Baby's mind right then. I could tell that by that terrified little whimper and that touch upon my arm.

I went rocketing out of that cave, and I went in to attack because I knew that was my only chance. Surprise sometimes gives an advantage.

What I wanted above everything else was to occupy that gorilla and give Baby a chance to escape without being seen. Sometimes Joseph Phineas Heggy has quite a streak of chivalry in him.

I guess the gorilla didn't see me coming. I guess if he had seen me he would have knocked my head off. As it was I broke my fist trying to knock his chin over the top of his head. Anyway, it felt as if I broke it. I must have damaged him, even though it felt as though I'd tried to knock a hole in this rocky wall. His head went back and he seemed to stagger a couple of strides. I came back at him, and I still had the advantage because he was between me and the light, and I fought with the black room as my background. I tried to knock him out with a few quick slams to the stomach, but with the first one-two I knew I was wasting my time.

Those stomach muscles had been developed so that they had the resistance of concrete — reinforced concrete!

Then the gorilla grabbed me and threw me over his shoulder. It did one good thing — it made him turn to come after me and then his back was to that rocky cavern and the girl had chance to run away.

The gorilla jumped on me and did a lot of painful things to my arms. Then I got a grip on his thumb and applied leverage in a scientific way and he went tottering off my body. He howled, and it was good to know that he was sensitive to pain.

He started to chase me, then, in and out the piles that supported the wall. It wasn't the kind of chase I'd recommend. There wasn't much light and there were plenty of shadows, I kept dodging from one pile to another, sometimes up to my ankles in stinking mud. He was much slower, but he was dogged and determined not to let me go.

Once he got me trapped where some boarding had been fixed across some piles. I had to fight my way out.

We slogged at each other, and we were gasping and grunting, but somehow I got round him and began to beat it again. This time I found the way to the open — I must have come on to the narrow pathway. I'd been pretty fast in my college days, and I streaked along that pathway faster than I'd ever gone on a football field.

That gorilla had the strength of me, but he didn't have speed. I got away from him then. But I was cursing as I ran. I'd expected that hideout under the wharf to be deserted this night, if only because I'd left the normal occupants happily drinking coffee out on the site. True, I'd guessed that Baby would turn up, but that had been part of my plan.

What hadn't been part of the plan was

that the gorilla should turn up. A cynical thought came to my mind that he wouldn't have turned up if Baby hadn't come padding along on her great elephant feet.

Maybe he'd seen Baby go under the piles and maybe he knew her menfolk were far away. Maybe he'd come after her with the happy idea of trying to find her in the darkness.

There were a lot of maybes, but that didn't get me anywhere. I was a marked man in this city and it was necessary for me to find a safe place in which to hole up. That hole in the rock wall under the wharf seemed no longer safe, and I'd lost Baby, who might have found me a quiet room somewhere.

I clambered up the rocky shore outside the wharf. The moonlight was strong upon me and I looked back at the shadowy darkness in which was the gorilla. I didn't linger. If that gent got his mitts on me I'd not live to see morning.

I went the only way I could go. I climbed up to the end of that alley, the one I'd walked along so recently. It seemed deserted now. a narrow street of low, tumbling, silent dwellings.

I started to hurry along, clinging to the shadowy side of the street.

A hand with a grip like the grab we had out on the site took hold of my shoulder and almost lifted me off the sidewalk.

Again I started to swing instinctively, and then I found myself up against something soft and I knew this was no enemy. It was Baby.

Baby had been hiding in a deep doorway, and when I came hurrying up she'd simply dragged me in by her side.

I caught the flash of her eyes and then the white of her teeth, and I thought she was a cheerful-looking jessie. We didn't speak. We crouched together, shrinking as far as possible into the shadow of that doorway. I heard the crinkle of transparent packaging, and I knew Baby hadn't run away without her precious nylons.

I could feel the warmth of her mighty body as we huddled together, and I was so close and so still that I could hear her heart pounding. It was a heart built to proportion, and it thumped with the rhythmical pounding of the steam hammer we had out at the site. Only, there seemed more power behind Baby's heart.

For all her grin I could feel she was trembling. She was terrified of being caught out by that Turkish male. I patted her bare arm in the darkness, and then we both froze into stillness for that gorilla had walked into the moonlight right before us.

He was a heavy, lowering brute, with his shaggy head sticking forward as his eyes searched the darkness suspiciously. The rags that covered his body seemed only to emphasise its giant strength, and his arms were swinging at his side with the fingers seeming to be clawing at my throat already.

He stood there right before us, and we didn't dare breathe. Plainly he was a mighty puzzled gorilla.

He'd gone after Baby and seen her disappear into that rocky cavern. The next thing she seemed to have changed into a man who jumped out and hit him painfully.

He was probably dazed from that first punch of mine, and he hadn't worked it all out. Baby was lost to him for the moment, and his little soul cried out for sight of the man who had socked him so painfully on the jaw.

That's what was in his mind, I guess. He stood there a long time, and we thought he must have seen me dodge into a doorway. But at length he began to pad softly along the street, and we clung there together in the darkness and watched until he disappeared round the far comer.

Clinging to Baby didn't seem a hardship, and I guess she got as much out of it as I did.

We even came apart with a bit of reluctance when the gorilla left the alley. But we finally came out from the doorway and that Turkish girl, with her arms full of packaged nylons, dropped her eyes modestly when the light fell on her face. There were things she could do in the darkness that made her blush when the light was upon her.

I thought hard and then came up with the Turkish I'd learnt from the book. I asked her, 'Find me a safe place where I can sleep.'

She was cute and tumbled to it quickly

what I wanted. She stood for a moment in the moonlight, very sturdy, her mighty legs and bare feet placed firmly apart, and I saw her pleasant, peasant face deep in thought.

After a while she smiled at me, and then said something rapidly in Turkish. I didn't understand, but when she started to pad along the street I came behind her.

At the end of the alley was a square that was quite busy at this time of night. There were Turkish cafés around it, a type of café patronised by dockside workers. They were solidly male, as always in these cafés, and they were out in the moonlight on the broad sidewalks at their tables. I let the girl get ahead of me on the crowded pavement, because she wouldn't want to be seen with me.

It wasn't a nice feeling, walking among that crowd; because I knew many must be U.N.P. supporters and I knew that I wasn't in favour with any of them. By now, probably, their newspapers would be putting up an intensive propaganda to convince their supporters and the world at large that a wretched American had bumped off their beloved leader.

I didn't bring any attention on myself, in spite of my misgivings. Evidently everyone was too concerned about his business to look closely at the tall stranger who strode in their midst.

The girl went to a doorway that looked sinisterly dark and let into a tall old building that fronted onto the square. I followed her inside. I only hoped there wasn't a gorilla waiting in the passage.

I saw Baby's mighty, muscular legs disappearing up a moonlit staircase, and I followed after her. She kept on climbing, and I thought we'd come out on the roof any minute.

But then she stopped outside a door on a passage that was lit only by streaming moonlight. It was an uninspiring passage, full of shadows and dirt. She knocked on the door and inside someone grumbled angrily and then came over and opened the door.

I saw a small man, a youngish man with jet-black hair set in neat waves. He had very bright eyes and a sharply intelligent face.

He wasn't a Turk I was sure, and I guessed he'd be an Armenian.

His bright eyes looked at Baby and then looked at me and were full of interest immediately. Baby, clutching those shiny packages of nylons spoke rapidly and in a shrill voice at him. I knew she was embarrassed and made nervous because she was seen with me, but she was a good girl and was trying to help a friend. The Armenian flashed a brilliant smile at me, and started to nod his head. I felt it was time I came in on the conversation.

I said, 'You speak English?'

'Perfectly, goddamn,' he answered promptly. That was a relief.

I said, 'Well, brother, are you going to help me?'

He held out his hand for money. I pulled out a pile of jack and waved it before him. I said, 'I've got plenty. You don't need to worry about that. You fix me and keep quiet about me and you'll make more money than you've had in a long time.' He nodded vigorously, and I was pretty sure I'd found a good ally.

Baby was smiling in relief now, as if she felt that my money had performed more than her tongue could have done.

The Armenian came out onto the passage. He was wearing wooden-soled sandals and he went clip-clopping along the bare boards until he came to a room at the end of the passage. The noise of the traffic in the square grew louder, and I could see the lights below as we stood by a window at the end of the passage.

He opened a door and walked in. A match spluttered and he lit an oil lamp. After a minute the small yellow flame seemed to be brilliantly bright and I was able to see the room he'd led me into.

It was like a Victorian museum. It was stuffed full of heavy furniture, mostly useless, and there were glazed china shepherds and shepherdesses all over the place. There was also a bed in one corner — a double bed.

My eyes came away from that bed with its ornate iron metalwork and brass knobs on comer posts. I caught the grin on that little, wavy-haired Armenian's face. He looked from me to Baby, seeming to burst out of that thin, torn dress.

Baby caught that grin and understood what the Armenian was thinking. She jumped into action immediately, her nut-brown face growing furious and her eyes widening with anger. Her voice shrilled up louder than ever and if it hadn't been for those nylons in her arms she would have gone for him, I guess.

I didn't understand a word of what she was saying, but I got the drift. She was telling the Armenian she wasn't a girl like that.

She even padded across to the door to show how virtuous were her intentions. I said to the Armenian, 'We won't both be staying, bub.'

He looked surprised. Again his eyes flickered across to look at Baby, and there was a puzzled frown on his face.

Baby turned her head away so as not to meet the interest of his gaze. She lingered a moment longer, and I caught her eye and it was rather soft, as if she was remembering that moment when the nylons went to her head in the cavern under the wharf. Perhaps she was regretting her inhibitions; perhaps she was thinking there was a good idea behind double beds even if they were brass-knobbed.

I smiled at her as she started to go, and I said, very cordially, 'You come up and see me anytime, Baby.'

She went away rather quickly then, because the Armenian started to translate and I could see he was putting in words of his own. She remembered she was Turkish and that meant a lot, and she went off down the passage.

I slapped some jack into the Armenian's greasy hand. I figured I'd paid enough to buy his loyalty.

He seemed very pleased with his night's work, and didn't want to go.

I wanted to stretch out and rest and think. So I put my arm round his shoulders like I loved him, got him out through the door and closed it on his face.

I took off my shoes and stretched myself on that bed. I wanted to think, but above all I wanted to sleep. It was still early night, but I'd taken enough exercise that day to satisfy me. I lay there, with a warm night breeze blowing in through the open window, and I tried to think. Outside the noise rose up to my window, and it seemed to be increasing. Not so much the noise of traffic increasing, but the sound of men's voices raised in talk.

Not too far away, too, some Turkish woman was singing to café patrons. When a Turkish woman sings in traditional manner no one sleeps. They love it in Turkey, but to Western ears the sound's hideous.

I tried to think. The funny thing was my first thought was about the Rumanian and Baby. I was thinking, 'Twice I've been thwarted today!'

That made it record day, and I didn't like making those kind of records. Only once before in my life could I remember being cheated — it was when a husband walked in on us.

He was a two-timing husband, and it hadn't been on my conscience. But today's events were on my conscience.

I lay there, relaxing and letting the tiredness flow out of my limbs, and I thought of that Rumanian girl back at the hotel. It made me feel bad, to be lying there alone in a strange bed when I knew she'd be glad of company.

Then my thoughts jerked round to another aspect of the Rumanian girl. She was in a jam. She was depending on me for money to see her through this period when she was without.

I started to think how to get money to her, and I even thought of going there during the night and entering her room by the fire escape,

I knew I was kidding myself, though. It wasn't altogether concern for her lack of finance that put this idea of fire escapes into my head . . . and then I threw away the thought. It was as the boys had said. The U.N.P. would be watching that Rumanian, on the principle that a man can't keep away from a girl once he knows she's his for the asking. To return would be to invite suicide.

I frowned in the darkness. The noise outside was getting worse than ever. Someone seemed to be shouting, and every now and then there was a low, sullen murmur that seemed almost like applause. I didn't pay any attention to it for the moment.

I was trying to work out my next move. Finding a place to hide was just a temporary expedient. It gave me safety for the moment, but ultimately it did nothing to resolve my difficulties.

I stared up at the whitewashed ceiling and I thought: *Heggy, you've got to try to find the killer of Habib Pasha.*

But how to begin? To show myself in that city with millions of people on the watch for me wouldn't be healthy. I thought of Mustapha Agloul, that man whose back only I had seen out at the site. I was wishing I had seen his face, because Tony Geratta had put a theory into my mind and I wanted to test it . . .

The talking down in the square below was louder than ever. Clearly some mob orator was addressing a crowd and they were making a lot of noise to show they were in approval.

After a time it got so that I couldn't even lie on my bed in comfort. I swung my feet over the edge and sat up. I was thinking I'd sure picked a swell place for a quiet rest.

Then I padded in my stockinged feet across to the window, and I leaned on the crumbling, wooden sill and looked down.

There was a public meeting in progress down in the square below. All auto traffic had ceased and the entire space was solid with Turkish males. Women wouldn't attend a public meeting like this, of course.

The lighted cafés around the square were deserted, as their patrons went to listen to the speaker.

A man was standing on the roof of a car, addressing the crowd. It was his voice that had been disturbing me when I sought rest on my bed. There was some light on the square, shining onto the upturned faces of the audience as they looked at that tall figure, seeming taller because he stood high above them on that car.

He was doing a lot of impassioned oratory, and I recognised those gestures with the arms and the quick movement of the hands. Here was a mob orator, a man trained in whipping up the emotions of a crowd.

Listening to the quickening response of those spectators, I knew that he had them in the palm of his hand. He was getting them worked up to a state of animal fury.

One second later I realised against whom that fury was being directed. It was me — Joe P. Heggy.

For suddenly that orator on the sedan roof turned and for the first time light fell on his face.

And I almost fell out of that window in astonishment, because I was looking down at the face of the man who had stabbed Habib Pasha in the back.

# 5

## Politician Heggy

I didn't move from that window. I just stood there, gripping that woodwork of the window frame, and looking down onto that orator.

The draught seemed to increase suddenly on my face, and I stiffened, realising what it meant.

The door had opened behind me.

I heard it close very softly.

I came wheeling round, crouching, my fists balled ready for action. There was only moonlight in the room because I'd put out the lamp before lying on the bed. It left the far end of the room in shadow, and it was there that the door was. And leaning against that door was the shadowy shape of a man.

I said, 'Who in hell are you? What are you doing in my room?'

Then he moved forward, and I caught

the glint of light on oil waves, and I knew it to be the Armenian. I saw moonlight in his bright eyes, and I saw that his lips were parted in a smile, but there wasn't any mirth in it. He came slowly up to me and faced me in the moonlight that streamed through that open window. Outside a mighty, exulting roar rose from that crowd at something the orator had said.

The moonlight fell on that Armenian's handsome face, and then his lips moved and I heard him say, 'You know what was said just then?'

I shook my head.

'The speaker said that an American, Joe P. Heggy, must be caught wherever he is and lynched. He said that American assassins must not be protected by a false justice.'

I took out a cigarette. I said, handing him one, 'It sounds unhealthy for Joe P. Heggy. Good job there are no U.N.P. supporters about.'

The Armenian bent his head and accepted a light. The red flame lit up his face and I saw that his eyes were watching mine curiously. Then he seemed to smile broadly, and he said, 'I am a member of the U.N.P.'

I stopped smoking. 'What are you going to do?' The U.N.P. supporters had instructions to hand me over for a lynching. What would the Armenian do?

The Armenian shoved out his hand. He didn't say anything.

I sighed and brought out my jack. He wasn't a very loyal supporter, evidently, and my money would keep his mouth shut.

I gave him more dough, and he started to get assertive and wanted much more. I wasn't taking too much from a piker, and I told him so. There was a limit to how far I would go to keep his mouth shut.

He looked at the money in his hand and he must thought it was pretty good, anyway, for his face broke into a sunny smile. I'd be all right there, he said; he wasn't really a U.N.P. supporter. As an Armenian how could he be an Ultra-Nationalist? I guessed he was only in the party for what he could get out of it. I wanted him to earn that money. I took him to the window and I pointed down, and I asked him, 'See that guy? What's his name?'

I knew the answer before he gave it.

He said, in surprise, 'That's the new leader of the U.N.P.'

'Mustapha Agloul?'

He nodded. I started to nod, too, and I was cynical with it. Tony Geratta's theory had been right Habib Pasha had been removed because his second-in-command didn't want to play second to any man.

There was another man standing on that sedan beside Mustapha Agloul. He had his arm round Mustapha's shoulders, like a man alongside his best friend. Now Mustapha was taking a rest from stirring up this mob, and his loving friend had taken over from him. He seemed to be whipping the crowd into a fury, just as successfully as the new U.N.P. leader.

I was looking down and brooding and thinking. After a while I jerked, 'What's that guy beefing about?'

The cheerful Armenian gave me a commentary. 'He's just saying what Mustapha's been saying. That Turkey is for the Turks and no one else. That all foreigners should be excluded, and the damned American is the first to go.'

There was another savage outburst of applause from that great milling throng in the square beneath me.

I said, 'What did he say then to get them so worked up?'

'He demanded your death, that is all.' The Armenian was very off-handed about it. 'Anyway, it wasn't his death, so why worry? He's telling the mob to form up and march to your hotel and drag you out and lynch you.'

I put up my hand to stop the translation. I was getting tired of that word lynch. Down below there was a convulsive, surging movement among the crowd, and I saw that a way was being cleared for that sedan to drive through, presumably to lead a procession up to the hotel where I was supposed to be. Maybe I'd been smart in finding another place for the night.

Idly I said, 'Who's that little guy alongside Mustapha?'

The Armenian told me — 'Yusef Khilil.

He's No. 2 in the party now.'

I grunted. 'He came up the promotion ladder with Mustapha, then.' I thought I'd shock the Armenian. His everlasting grin got on my nerves a bit. I said, 'You know who killed Habib Pasha?'

That grin again. 'You?'

I pointed down to that sedan inside which Mustapha was riding alongside his loving comrade Yusef. I said, 'It was Mustapha Agloul. I saw him do it.'

I was disappointed. The Armenian didn't turn a hair. Instead he nodded vigorous agreement. I was surprised to hear him say, 'That's what a lot of U.N.P. members think.'

It was my turn to be astonished. I said, 'Then if that's what they're saying, why in heck are they wanting to lynch me?'

The Armenian walked back into the room, and shrugged his shoulders indifferently. He was a natural intriguer. 'Mustapha's the boss now. It doesn't matter what people think, they do what Mustapha tells them to do. He controls the party and you don't argue with a man in control like Mustapha.'

I thought of the strong-arm boys who had been sent to do me in — twice. I could see the Armenian's argument. If Mustapha controlled the strong-arm element in the party, then it wasn't healthy for people to voice their suspicions. Instead, it was a whole lot better for them if they jumped on the wagon and cheered whatever Mustapha said.

Then I began to think of Yusef Khilil, another politician. I did quite a lot of thinking in the space of a few seconds, and then I looked up and saw those very bright Armenian eyes on me.

I glanced below into the lighted square, and I saw that it was emptying as the excited U.N.P. supporters straggled off in procession after the sedan.

Then a thought struck me. I said, 'You got a telephone?'

The Armenian nodded vigorously and proudly. It surprised me. The top half of this building, anyway, didn't have electric light, and so it was a surprise to know they'd heard of the invention of the telephone.

I said, 'I want to use it. Come on,

brother, I want to get to bed.'

We went cautiously out on to the passage, because neither of us wished strange eyes to see an American in that curious situation. But the shadowy passage was deserted, and we made his room without any alarm.

It was another overcrowded room, but this time it was overcrowded with packing cases and cartons, and seemingly thousands of bottles. I sat down at the telephone — a spidery-looking, pre-war German installation. I decided I couldn't use it and I asked the Armenian to get me a number. He did it quickly, in about ten minutes of much shouting.

During this time I'd picked up one of the bottles. It was filled with black-looking liquid, and I opened it and sniffed it and it smelled vile. I couldn't read the label because it was in Turkish, so I said, 'What is your line of business, brother?'

It took him some time to think of a suitable explanation in English. Then, holding that telephone to his ear and grinning larger than ever, he said, 'The old men like it. It makes them young again.' And he gave a sudden quick pantomime that told better than words what he meant by young.

He was generous. 'Go on,' he urged. 'You get round a bottle yourself, Mr. Heggy.'

I shook my head. 'The Heggy's never needed this stuff,' I said, deprecatingly.

While waiting for the number he took the bottle out of my hand and drank half the contents. He smacked his lips over it, too, as if he enjoyed the stuff he peddled.

He announced, brightly, 'Tonight I see my girl. It is good to have some of that liquor inside you when you meet your girl.'

I didn't argue with him, and then a voice came through the wire that wasn't the telephone operator's.

I got on to the 'phone. It was B.G. Before I could say anything except, 'That you?' he jumped into his stride and started to babble at me.

'Where are you, Heggy? For God's sake, I'm coming right over to you.'

I said, 'Like hell you are. What's biting you?'

He said, 'It's that Dunkley woman — '

I sighed. I said, 'Is she still chasing you?'

B.G. poured out a flood of words. I gathered that that frustrated little English woman wasn't leaving him alone any of the time. Wherever he went about that hotel she was trotting after him. All the time she was so timid and apologetic, and seeming not daring to touch his sleeve, but all the time she was whispering for him to come out into the darkness to see the lovely Bosporus,

'But I'm not going.' B.G.'s voice had a quiver in it. 'A man's not safe with a woman like that about. She's not soft and nervous at all. She's a brazen and shameless woman, and if I got out into the darkness with her, heaven knows what she'd do.'

I said coarsely a lot of other people could make a good guess.

B.G. said, stiffly, 'You don't understand. The trouble with you, Heggy, is you're naturally crude. You've never thought of saving yourself for the moment when the right woman comes into your life.'

I could even picture that fat face blinking and looking virtuous behind its glasses at that priggish remark. I thought I'd help him out. I said, 'Don't go out with her now, anyway. There's a mob of several thousand Ultra-Nationalists heading for the hotel right now, and I'm telling you the way they feel they're going to tear every American they meet into cent-size pieces of dead meat.'

That upset him almost as much as being chased by the chaste Miss Dunkley. I told him to warn the other boys, and I suggested he rang for the police so that they'd be there before the rioting broke out. The U.N.P. were in a dangerous mood that night.

Then I told him why I'd rung him. 'Look, B.G., you've got to do me a favour. You know that Rumanian girl-friend of mine?'

He knew of her. Evidently the boys had been giving him the details.

'Go to her from me, and give her some money. The gal's broke.'

He didn't like it. It didn't sound nice to him. Why was I giving her money?

I told him that was something between me and the Rumanian gal. But I said I was well satisfied with my side of the bargain. That made B.G. get more and more priggish than ever. Plainly he felt that he was going to be soiled by participating in this arrangement, as he described it.

'What is her name, anyway, Heggy?'

I told him I didn't know. I'd forgotten to ask her. At that he exploded. He said it wasn't decent, trying to make love to a girl and not even know her name.

He got me exasperated because there seemed no logic in what he was saying. I said, 'The hell, you don't need visiting cards when you take a yen for a girl!' Then I told him he'd better get around to that girl pretty quickly, or I'd fix him for a lot of trouble. He knew I meant it. He was only the boss, after all.

Just to upset him a bit more I gave him a message to give to the girl. 'You tell her not to be surprised if she wakens some morning and finds Heggy already there.'

Then I hung up. The Armenian had enjoyed the conversation. As I rose to leave the room he waved towards those thousands of youth-revivers and said in a scornful manner, 'They don't beat nature, huh?'

I said, 'They're a darned long way from being the right thing. Heggy won't ever need 'em.'

I went up to that room of mine, and fixed the door so that no one could get in without waking me. Then I stripped off and got into a bed that made music every time I turned, but it was comfortable.

When I awoke it was to see that door coming open under the impetus of a powerful shove. I half came out of bed and then sank back.

It was Baby.

She pushed again and the chair came apart from the handle under which it had been propped. Baby came into the room, but she was shy this morning, and she left the door open as if she thought she might have to run for it. Her mood had certainly changed considerably from that moment of nylon-induced passion.

The sun was streaming in at that window, already hot, though it couldn't have been more than half an hour risen. It flooded that high, attic room with cheerful sunlight, and it lit up that girl by the doorway almost as if she were in the glare of a spotlight.

And I saw at once the reason for her shyness, for the flush on her pleasant brown face.

She'd come to show me her new pretty things.

On those mighty, but not unshapely legs were nylons. This day, though, they weren't wrinkled and drooping as they had been when first she had pulled them hastily on. Now they were suspended, or at least fixed in the way they should be fixed, and they slimmed off her legs and made them look infinitely more graceful. And she was wearing shoes.

I thought they were probably borrowed shoes, and they must have hurt her like hell, because she hadn't the feet for that kind of shoe. But she was proud of them; they were the finishing touch.

I lifted my eyes and met her bright brown ones, and there was appeal in them. She wanted to be sure she was admired.

My eyes fell on that sun-bleached, shapeless rag of a dress she wore — a dress that was thin and clung to her.

I saw the rent in her dress, and she hadn't been able to fix it. She was a nice girl, was Baby, and I felt like being big-hearted to her again.

I started to get out of bed, and then I remembered I wasn't dressed for company.

I said, 'Baby, you sure look swell.' And I shook my head admiringly and let my eyes linger on those mighty limbs of hers. She didn't understand, but she gathered that I was in approval. It pleased her and her face broke into a pleasant smile of happiness. I saw bright, even teeth — teeth big enough to eat a man, I thought. And yet attractive teeth. When she smiled her eyes nearly disappeared.

I said, 'I'll be hungry, Baby. You get me some food.' I pantomimed, and grabbed my pants and gave her some kurus. She understood.

She picked up her shoes and carefully took off those nylons and left them inside my room. Evidently nylons were to look at, but weren't to wear around the place. She padded off to get me food, and while she was away I got dressed and thought of the plans I had made in the few minutes before going to sleep the previous night.

Baby came back, and she had brought me plenty to eat. There was a good big salad, and though that isn't usual for a Western breakfast, it was right enough to eat. And there was native bread that had flavour in it, and she'd brought some tiny cups of coffee. She brought half a dozen, because she was a wise gal and knew an American didn't want an egg cup full of coffee. There was also a glass of water to go with the coffee, in true Turkish fashion.

I saw her looking at the food and so I waved and said, 'Help yourself, Baby.'

She took some persuading because she was timid of foreign males. But after a while she forgot to be timid, and she came and sat on the bed with me and we ate together. We couldn't talk and understand each other, but I kept talking and she kept laughing and it wasn't a bad breakfast at all. When it was over she went and climbed into her nylons. It was the most wonderful thing that had ever come into her life, I guess. She just couldn't stop fingering them.

I'd got work for her to do, though, so I started to do a bit more pantomiming. I made sketchy indications of garments that came a little higher than stockings and said, 'Nylons.'

She got me. Her eyes lit up, and she nodded vigorously. She was in for everything now. So I said, 'You take a letter for me up to my hotel?'

She understood when I got out a pen and wrote a note to Marty. When I put the address of the hotel on it she must have recognised it, for she nodded vigorously again and accepted the letter. I knew she'd deliver it to Marty, and I guessed she'd be a safe messenger for me.

She seemed reluctant to leave. Perhaps she'd got back some of the old urge because of the mateyness of our break-fasting. She lingered by the door and she threw roguish glances at me,

The Armenian saved me. Suddenly he was right there at the door, and the expression in his bright eyes was sufficient to fill Baby with indignation. She shrilled something angrily at him, and no doubt was denying everything. Then she hurried away down the passage.

The Armenian sauntered in. He gave me a suggestive look and said, 'You no need my liquor, huh?'

I didn't follow up that line of conversation. I asked, 'What happened to the U.N.P. last night?'

He shrugged. 'A couple of them got killed. They tried to get the Americans out of the hotel to kill them. But someone had got the police there, and there was some fighting, and our police aren't too gentle.'

I licked my lips at that. I was thinking this didn't help to make things any better for Americans, in Turkey. Two more deaths would be laid at their door. I thought, 'Blast it, that Mustapha Agloul's got to be shown up for the two-timing murderer he is!'

I said to the Armenian, 'I want to meet Yusef Khilil. Will you bring him here?'

That did startle the Armenian. His eyes

went big and bright and then he said, 'You'll die for certain.'

I said. 'I'll risk it.'

He didn't like the idea, and he put up another argument. 'They'll kill me for hiding you.'

I got tired with him and told him he was selfish. I was willing to risk my life, why shouldn't he? He didn't seem convinced, so I brought out all I had left of my jack. It talked powerful hard in my favour, that money.

I gave him his instructions. 'You meet Yusef and tell him you've got a big business proposition. If he's the politician I think him to be, that'll bring him here. But don't mention that I am here, or he might get scared.'

The Armenian departed reluctantly. While he was away I went to use his telephone, and I sat amidst that array of bottles and waited while an English-speaking operator got me through to Marty Dooley. I noticed another empty bottle on the table by the telephone, and I guessed that the Armenian had been at his own liquor even so early in the morning.

I sniffed the empty bottle experimentally. I made a guess at the contents. It was raw alcohol and aniseed.

I thought that if it didn't make the old men younger, enough of this stuff and they wouldn't care, anyway. I thought maybe the Armenian had taken a stiff shot himself before going to see Yusef Khilil.

About a quarter of an hour later Marty spoke to me. That's pretty good for the Istanbul telephone department. Marty blew up when he heard my voice. That redhead was in a raging temper.

I gathered that it wasn't safe for Americans to leave their hotels, and there was a strong police guard making sure they didn't. The work out at the site had come to a standstill, and that was making Marty hopping mad. We were falling behind on a tight schedule.

I got tired in the end and told him to quit beefing, and then his anger exploded at me.

'You're no trouble-buster. You're just a goddamned trouble-maker. You keep your eyes closed next time you see someone getting a knife in his back!'

I told him he was unreasonable. He shot back that we couldn't afford to get embroiled in local politics and I ought to know that. He started making sarcastic remarks about trouble-busting again, so I talked back at him.

I said, 'If you shut your face a second, Marty, I'll tell you something. I'm figuring on busting this trouble mighty soon. We'll all be out on the site again soon, and work will resume where we left off.'

He got a bit mollified at that, but I refused to tell him anything more of the plan in my mind. I was a trouble-buster, I kept repeating, and I would bust this particular piece of trouble within forty-eight hours.

After that it was a pleasanter conversation. Marty knew me, and knew I didn't shoot my mouth easily. He'd seen me in action too many times before.

I asked him about B.G.

'B.G. daren't leave his room,' Marty chuckled. 'He's in a terrible way.'

'Lav?' I asked softly.

'Lav,' he repeated. 'The boys hadn't

anything else to do last night, and they got little Lavinia outside a few strong drinks. After that she didn't give a damn about appearances. She went after B.G., and he had a hell of a time. The last I saw of her she was trying to get into his room after him.'

It made me feel happy to think of that slob of a boss of mine being on the run like that. I approved of the boys' wicked sense of humour, and I said so.

Marty got back to the subject of the U.N.P. Things had been hectic around the hotel, but the police had been at their best in quelling the disturbance.

Marty's description of the affair was quite graphic.

He told me that the U.N.P. had ordered a strike of all workers for that afternoon. This affair was rapidly becoming a national problem, and for a few moments I wished to hell I'd never looked out of that plane window and glimpsed the killing. I thought: That comes of trying to get close to a woman.

Marty hung up after a while, when he found I hadn't anything to tell him. He was going to get stinking drunk with the boys, because that was the only way he could forget the damage done to his precious schedule by this U.N.P. hostility.

I hefted a bottle of the Armenian's Youth Restorer, and Marty's talk of getting drunk put ideas into my own mind. I even tried a drink from the bottle, but that aniseed flavouring was too much for me. I spat the fiery liquid out and went back to my own room, cautiously making sure that the dingy landing was deserted before doing so.

I'd been there about an hour when I heard someone coming along the passage. It was Baby. She was barefooted this time, and in a sweat because she had hurried all the way from the hotel. Marty had given her some of my clothes. I figured I'd need a new shirt, at least, for what was in my mind.

Baby wanted to stop, and maybe she had it in mind to play with this American who promised such wonderful things in nylon. But I wanted to change and look more presentable for when Yusef Khilil arrived, and when I started to peel off my soiled shirt modesty overcame the Turkish girl and she went out the way she had come.

I was a very wonderful kind of person to Baby.

I'd changed and shaved with the razor that I'd asked for, when more footsteps were heard out in the passage. I strained my ears, and thought there were at least two people approaching. I went out and stood behind the door. I couldn't put treachery from the Armenian out of my mind.

He was a nice guy, as nice guys go, but some nice guys go much too far.

There was a knock on the door, a furtive sound that hinted at intrigue. I called out, 'Walk right in.'

The Armenian walked in. I saw his back. He started to twist in surprise, because the room seemed empty. A man walked in right behind him, a Turk by his looks.

He was growing old, and out of breath because of the many stairs he had had to climb. I had a feeling he was in a bad temper, also.

He was stocky, long-bodied and short-legged, with his head curiously sunk into his shoulders. In profile he had a face that mama couldn't love — it was big in the nose, and fleshy round the chin.

I closed the door and shot a bolt. That was to keep out anyone else not on the programme.

Both turned at the sound behind them. The Armenian's eyes lit up with relief, and that everlasting, brilliant smile of his shone forth.

Yuself Khilil didn't smile. Instead that yellow, lined face seemed to go stiff, as if with shock and fear.

His brown eyes, which protruded slightly at normal times, seemed almost to glare with apprehension at the tall American who had shut the door on him.

I saw that he knew me — or guessed my identity — at once. He turned to the Armenian and he began to talk with his arms and shout angrily at the same time, but all the time he kept one eye on me. After all, I was a man who was supposed to have slipped a knife into his boss's back. It might be a habit with me, he was thinking.

I lifted my hand. I said, 'Brother,

you've got it wrong. This isn't any sort of trap.' For I guessed what he was shouting at the cheerful Armenian.

I said, 'I sent for you because we can do business together — plenty business. You understand English?' That thought came to me belatedly.

I was relieved when that sunken head nodded.

There was a thoughtful look in those brown eyes that showed the whites nearly all the way round. They were fixed on me, and there was calculation in them.

He was noting the good suit of clothes I wore, and no doubt he was remembering the fabulous wealth of these Americans who came to his country. Being a politician his thoughts no doubt kept coming back to the supposed wealth of America.

I walked away from the door, and that gave him confidence. He could, if he had wanted, have gone out through the door and onto the passage. The fact that he didn't, but instead walked across and sat on a stiff-backed chair by the foot of that brass-knobbed bed which had been made in Victorian England, showed that he was willing to talk turkey.

He said, 'You are — ?'

He wanted it confirmed. 'I'm Joe P. Heggy.'

I sat down on the edge of the bed, my hands clasped before me. I looked at him and thought,

'You're treacherous enough for anything.'

He said, 'My party are out looking for you. You have caused a lot of trouble. Mr. Heggy.'

But he called me 'mister'.

I said, 'You know damned well I never killed Habib Pasha. You know it's just convenient, from your party's point of view, that the crime should be saddled on the Americans. You want to come to power and you're trying to do it on a popular issue — Turkey for the Turks, and the hell with every other national!

'But maybe you haven't got this figured out quite straight, Mr. Khilil. Maybe it would pay you better to try to find the truth.' I put an emphasis on the word pay, and I could see the interest blossoming in his brown, bead-like eyes.

I spoke with brutal frankness. 'Habib Pasha was stabbed in the back by your present leader, Mustapha Agloul. I saw him do it when I came in to land at the airport.'

He didn't seem any more shocked by the statement than the Armenian, but his bright brown eyes registered doubt. 'I can hardly believe your story, Mr. Heggy.'

'You mean, you don't think I could have spotted the incident from a landing aircraft, and seen the face of the murderer so that I could identify it?' I waved my hand. 'You forget your doubts, brother. It'll pay you, anyway. Just you ask anyone who has done much flying how much they can see from a low-flying plane that's fluttering in to land.'

He was willing to believe me. He started to nod his head. His eyes were hard upon me, wanting to know my proposition.

I leaned forward and spoke earnestly. 'Look Yusef, that guy Mustapha isn't the kind of fellow you should have as leader. I figure you'd be a much more suitable head of a political party.'

It was jam and molasses, but these guys are suckers for flattery. He lapped it up. I could even see the calculation in his eyes as he thought of himself as the leader of the U.N.P. — and drawing the leader's pay packet.

'I have no doubt you are right, Mr. Heggy.' He seemed to blow himself out in a sudden access of importance. 'There are many in my party who have long considered Mustapha Agloul unfit for the high position he holds. In fact only a few hours before his death Habib Pasha had told us that Mustapha had to go.'

I nodded sagely. The whole thing was coming clearer now. Before, I had thought that Mustapha Agloul had murdered his chief merely in order to step into his shoes. But now it seemed there had been a greater need for murder — Mustapha Agloul had been on the point of being 'purged'!

When the politician is in such a position, he does desperate things. It had spurred Mustapha Agloul on to — murder! It had been bold, but it had come off, for he had been able to assume leadership before he could be thrown out of the party. Now, as leader they couldn't throw him out.

I was remembering those strong-arm boys who had come to attack me upon the new leader's orders. They would enforce Mustapha Agloul's orders.

I said to Yusef, 'All you've got to do, Yusef, is to stand up at your next meeting and publicly denounce Mustapha Agloul.'

Yusef looked quickly at the Armenian. He said, 'You don't understand our politics.'

'You mean you think you'd be courting suicide to speak against your new leader?'

'He controls the militant section of our party.'

I got impatient. I said, 'Look, Yusef, he can't do a thing to you if you denounce him in public. Get yourself a nice big crowd like last night's out there — ' I nodded towards the square below my window — 'And you'll have so many supporters right away that Mustapha's strong-arm boys won't dare do anything to you,'

He could see the force of my argument.

Probably he was picturing himself on the roof of a sedan denouncing Mustapha Agloul as an unscrupulous and treacherous careerist, prepared to kill his leader in order to advance himself.

And he was seeing in his mind's eye the reaction to his words. There would be violent anger in an instant, because the rank and file of any political party is much the same anywhere. They dislike to see men climbing at the expense of others — especially at the expense of other people's lives. Yusef would find himself immediately with a majority of supporters.

He licked his lips, and considered the problem, but I could see he hadn't guts enough to do it. So I played my trump card. I said, 'You fix your meeting like last night's in the square below. When you've denounced Mustapha Agloul, I'll get on to that car roof beside you and I'll testify to what I saw.'

It startled them. It sounded too fantastically reckless to believe.

The Armenian exclaimed, 'You would never reach the car. They would tear you limb from limb!'

I said, 'They're my limbs. I'll take the risk. I figure they'll be so interested in hearing Yusef's statement, they'll never even see me as I shove my way through the crowd up to that car. And once I'm up there alongside you, Yusef, they won't touch me.'

I knew crowd psychology. If I had guts enough to show myself and demand justice for the dead Habib, I'd find a good half or more of that crowd rooting for me. I was willing to back my psychology, anyway.

Yusef made up his mind. 'If you make that promise, I'll denounce Mustapha Agloul.'

I could see his eyes glistening. It would be a big moment for him, even though only a few hours ago he had been standing in public with his arm round his comrade's shoulders.

I said, softly, 'You'll be a mighty influential man, then, Yusef. You'll be able to turn off this hate-campaign that your party's setting up against Americans.'

He was looking at me very hard. Suddenly he said something in Turkish and the Armenian went out. He went reluctantly, but evidently he was under orders. When the Armenian was in the passage outside, Yusef said, 'Now you can talk freely. What is your proposition?'

He was completely blunt and bold about it.

I said, 'You tone down this anti-American propaganda, and I'll see that Gissenheim's make a nice, fat contribution to the U.N.P. funds.'

He was startled. 'But we couldn't take American money!'

I shook my head sadly. I said, 'It doesn't need to go to the party funds. It can go into your pocket and you can use it the way you think fit.'

I'd seen politicians bought before today, and I knew I could buy this one. It was a dirty game to play, but if it put an end to our troubles out on the new airfield it was worth a bit of graft and I knew Berny would okay it.

I saw him begin to nod. He murmured, 'Of course I will not use it personally.'

I said, heavily, 'Of course not.'

He grew expansive, 'You do not

understand how deeply we feel about nationalism in Turkey. Personally, I think sometimes we go too far.' That was his let out so that he could accept Gissenheim's graft.

I slapped him on the back. I wanted to slap his treacherous fat neck so hard that it broke. But I just gave a Heggy smile, and said, 'Sure, sure, I don't understand your politics. But I figure if your people took to ball games a bit more they sure would feel better with themselves.'

He smiled. 'I have heard of your ball games. What are they like?'

I said, 'You put a lot of men on to a field and they try to tear each other apart. If they aren't vigorous enough, the crowd howl for them to take the referee apart. We call it sport.'

He was moving to the door. He asked, quickly, 'Any money in sport?'

'Promoting it? Plenty.'

As he was going out he told me it was too late to fix the meeting for that night, but he would arrange things for the night after.

He also told me the papers were

demanding that I should come out of hiding, because the police were wanting to take me out of the country.

'They say your presence in Turkey will be inflammatory.' It was a good word for a politician.

'They think more trouble will follow if you stay on in Istanbul.'

I nodded. But I told him I would go out of Turkey when I'd fixed the Habib Pasha killing where it belonged — and that wasn't on Joe P. Heggy.

He went and the Armenian returned. He wasn't smiling. In fact he was a very sullen man. I knew what was griping him.

'You're kind of sore because you didn't hear what we planned?' The Armenian didn't say anything.

He just stood at the window and looked out, and I had a feeling that he could become mighty awkward if he wasn't smoothed down.

So I told him the truth. 'I just bought Yusef Khilil. That's the kind of politician you've got.'

He turned round then, his eyes smiling eagerly.

'How much did you give him?'

I said, 'I gave him nothing — but I promised him a lot.'

That Armenian started to laugh then, and he thought it a hell of a good joke. To his mind he was quite certain that I was planning a double-cross on Yusef, and he was quite prepared to appreciate it as the kind of thing that should happen to a crooked politician. I let him go on thinking it, though I meant every word I'd said to Yusef. I'm no double-crosser, and I'd see that Gissenheim's gave him the softener that I'd promised.

I only hoped it wouldn't do him any good.

Baby kept coming up that day, and I was glad the Armenian never left me. She came in useful to bring up coffee for us, and we passed away the hours playing the Turkish national game of backgammon.

I knew what Baby wanted. She was waiting for me to come out with those other nylon underthings I'd promised, and she would have liked to have had me alone, I figured.

But Baby was a bit too much woman

for one man, and I gave her no encouragement that day.

In the evening, however, when darkness came and moonlight streamed in at my lofty window I began to regret the way I'd treated Baby. It gets intolerable to a man of my temperament to have to stay put in one place for any long time. I'd been in this small room longer than I liked, and I was in a worse temper than Marty Dooley long before midnight.

I tried sleeping because there was nothing to sit up for, but it didn't work. Baby would have been a blessing. The Armenian had gone out with the darkness to deliver some stock, so far as I could make out. He seemed to have got round more of it himself, and he wasn't very steady going down the stairs.

I wasn't too happy about that load of alcohol he was carrying under his skin. A man in that condition sometimes grows boastful — and it was my neck that was at stake, not his.

I started to follow up that line of thought, though I knew deep down I was kidding myself. I thought: He might open his big, blabber-mouth, and any time now some of the U.N.P. strong-arm boys might come creeping up those stairs.

I was bored and in a bad temper and I started to think up all the reasons why I shouldn't stay in that moonlit room. I knew the risks I would take if I went out into Istanbul's streets, but I just couldn't stay alone up there any longer.

Shortly before midnight I went down into that square with its many cafés and many more patrons, and all of them male. I kept to the darker parts of the square, and Istanbul doesn't go in much for street lighting, anyway. I figured I would get by unless someone actually bumped into me.

My feet took me the shortest route back to the hotel — and the lovely Rumanian girl. Before I'd gone a quarter of a mile I stopped kidding myself, too.

I knew why I'd left that attic room. It wasn't fear of an Armenian talking alcoholically. It was the lure of a girl — the Rumanian girl.

When I'd stopped kidding myself and I knew what I was going after that night, I started to walk at a faster pace than before. It was a good way from the dockside quarter up to the heights of Pera, where my hotel was, but walking did me no harm and there was no question of trying to take one of the old rattle-trap trams or hail a taxi. I wouldn't have lived long if I had done.

For that was something I was realising all the time. That to most people in Istanbul I was a murderer walking at large.

It wasn't a nice feeling to think that any moment someone might come and try to do me in on the theory that I had killed a man.

# 6

Hot fingers!

I'd got down to one cigarette — that, in fact, had been one of the excuses I had used to myself to get me out of that room. I must get some cigarettes, I had argued.

I walked across that broad iron bridge that spans the Golden Horn, and then, feeling safe now that I was over the water, I stuck my cigarette between my lips and flipped my lighter.

Two men came out of the shadows almost immediately. I had shielded the flame so that I was confident my face hadn't been revealed. But those two bozos were coming straight for me — no mistake about that.

More, they were so close to me that there was no chance of running away.

One of them spoke rapidly in Turkish. I didn't understand what was being said, but then, in the darkness, I saw a finger point at the lighter I was just putting away, and I got it in one.

They were asking to see my licence for my cigarette lighter. In Turkey the match-making industry is a Government monopoly, and to protect it they permit people to use lighters only if they pay a tax. To be found using a lighter without a licence is a punishable offence.

I had no licence, but as a foreign national I didn't need one. But if I started to explain that, they'd get interested in my voice and would take a look at me, and from what I'd heard the entire Istanbul police force was on the lookout for me.

I jumped quickly between them and shoved them apart as I crashed through. I wasn't going to be taken off to any Istanbul police station, there to be packed aboard a plane and sent out of the country so that I wouldn't get hurt. I could see a way of clearing myself and of effecting justice, and I intended to hang on to Istanbul a little while longer, anyway.

They didn't like being shoved about,

and I heard hoarse, angry voices and then the rapid pad-pad of leather slapping the sidewalk as they started to run after me.

But I'd been all day resting, and I could run like the devil when I chose. Right then I chose.

But I was having to run straight towards a busy, well-lighted crossroads, with plenty of traffic and much electric lighting.

The cops — because of course they were plain-clothes police — were shouting now, and it was attracting attention where the busy sidewalk lay ahead of me. I decided not to go that way the moment I saw an alley dropping down to my left.

I turned and ran into darkness. I didn't know where I was going, but I had no intention of running on to that lighted thoroughfare. Then the narrow, almost lampless street began to climb steeply, and I knew that at least I was heading now for Pera. The police were a long way behind now, and I started to go more easily. Then the street curved and I found myself running on to that busy thorough-fare again. There was even a bunch of low-deck trolley cars crashing by at that moment.

I was panting, and I dropped to a walk and tried to keep to the shadows. I got out on to that thoroughfare in time to see a car come charging up the hill towards me, with a big Storm Trooper-like cop hanging on to the footboard.

I hesitated. I was in a jam. That alley was blank all the way along it, without any side turnings, and those two cops were pounding up the hill after me. Now this car was bearing down upon me and bringing another cop on to my trail. For a second it seemed as though I was trapped.

I ran right across that busy street, with its uneven cobblestones and deep-rutted tram track. For right opposite me I'd seen a passageway that was surely too narrow for a car to squeeze in. It was my only chance — to even things up by at least making automobile pursuit useless.

I saw a crowd chasing up the hill after that car, and I heard the cop shouting and pointing at me. No doubt about it, Istanbul was on the trail of, as they thought, a dangerous foreign murderer.

Now I knew that if I didn't keep ahead of that crowd, it wouldn't be just a case of being marched off to a police station.

I'd be torn apart if the good citizens of Istanbul laid their mitts on me.

That sure put wings to my feet. I went rushing up that winding passageway between buildings with deep shadowy doors — private residences, I supposed, but all with their doors closed at that time of night.

Behind me men poured into the passage and came after me as hard as they could go. I began to think there wasn't a chance for me.

But there was — a most unexpected chance.

I ran out of that alley, and the moment I came out of it I knew where I was. I wasn't more than a few hundred yards from the back of my hotel, and I was facing a building that was familiar to everybody who came to Istanbul.

It was the headquarters of the Ultra-Nationalist Party.

There was a big procession of U.N.P.

supporters marching off in front of their headquarters. They were the strikers of that day out to stage a demonstration before they went back to work the following morning. There were thousands of them. All I did was to walk right in among them, and once I was in that procession, those cops and people panting up the passageway never had a chance of spotting the man they sought.

I didn't think the marchers in that procession would spot me, either. We were all packed so close together, and there weren't many lights along the route they had chosen. It turned out that the police had banned them from marching along any main street, and so they were forced to keep to the back ways and, as I say, Istanbul doesn't spend a lot of the taxpayers' money on street lighting.

And so I found salvation in the midst of the enemy. I just tramped along with them, and listened to their excited cheers and shouted slogans, and no one took a blind bit of notice of me.

I kept edging across the procession, so that eventually I was able to step out on the sidewalk right opposite from where I'd joined the crowd. When I realised how near I'd got to the hotel I dropped out of the demonstration. No one noticed my departure. I just walked away and that was that.

I let them go on, shadowy shapes and ghostly faces marching in disorderly manner down the narrow alley.

It did me another good turn, too, that demonstration. It emptied the streets in the vicinity of the hotel, because people like a free show anywhere, and they all went flocking to watch the U.N.P. march by.

I didn't go to the front of the hotel. It wasn't any good advertising my presence there. If I was seen entering the foyer, some bright alec would for sure go and tell the demonstrators, and they were in such numbers this night that for certain they'd take the hotel apart in order to get me.

Lynching is a good sport for mobs.

I clung to the shadows, and fortunately they were plenty. There weren't many people about and they took no notice of me that I could see, anyway.

I went round to the rear of the hotel, and I was looking for fire escapes, because I knew one ran right past the Rumanian girl's window. I was doing a lot of calculating, too, and I figured I could make the Rumanian girl's room at first go . . .

I would ask her for her name, first opportunity, I thought. It was getting clumsy even in my thoughts to call her 'the Rumanian'.

There was a stink of garbage, and some stray cats were fighting among the inevitable cans of refuse that stack behind any hotel. But the cats hadn't got anything against me so I didn't worry over them.

I found the fire escape. It was the kind that comes down under the weight of anybody descending, but no one was descending so that meant I'd have to jump up to catch it. I jumped and I got it and it came down with quite a noise, but I felt that that wouldn't bring anyone out enquiringly. At that late hour people mind their own business.

But I stood there, all the same, for five solid minutes, holding on to that ladder and watching around to see if anyone was coming towards me.

When I was sure I was safe I started to go up that ladder. I counted the floors, and then at last I felt pretty sure I was outside the window of the Rumanian girl.

Again I waited in the shadows, while the moonlight lit up the sides of the hotel to my left. There were lights on in some of the windows, and radio music from too many rooms. It was Radio Ankara, and Radio Ankara goes in a lot for singers, local variety. It makes the night hideous for American ears, anyway.

Nothing happened. No one moved. I took courage again and turned to the window. It wasn't fastened. I just pulled and it opened and I stepped inside.

There was plenty of light within that room — moonlight that came streaming in at a low angle. It threw the rear part of the room into shadow, but it also fell upon part of the bed. It didn't quite light up the bed — not all of it. Yet I could see that someone lay there under the cover of a single white sheet. You don't need more than that on a Turkish summer's evening.

I stood quite a long time looking into that room and listening to the sounds of the demonstrators in the distance. My eyes were watching the blackness beyond the bed, because shadows could spell danger for a man who was thought to be a murderer.

Then I started to go across that soft, carpeted floor towards the bed. When I was a couple of yards from it I had a sudden stabbing doubt.

You know how it happens. Suddenly you don't feel sure.

Until that moment I'd been certain that this was the lovely Rumanian girl's room, but now all at once I was unsure.

Illogically I thought: Maybe it might even be Lav! A sour grin came to my face in the darkness, thinking about it, because in her state of mind it wasn't safe for any man to go into her room.

Then I dismissed the thought. I had an idea, thinking back, that she was in a room next to the Rumanian's, but she wouldn't have a fire escape right outside her window, too.

I took two more strides and then I knew I'd made no mistake. That billowing mass of dark hair that flooded over the pillow could only belong to my beautiful Rumanian. I looked at her in the shadows where the moonlight failed to reach — and I realised that she was awake and looking at me. She had recognised me.

I didn't speak then. I knew I was welcome, if I'd had any doubts before, because she wouldn't have lain like that and kept quiet if she hadn't wanted me there.

I sat on the edge of the bed. Still we hadn't spoken. I felt her fingers reach out from behind me and stroke my arm. It was a soothing, caressing gesture.

There was an odour of perfume, and I guessed she'd just bathed.

And then someone knocked at the door.

We both stiffened, but didn't move. I saw the surprise in the girl's big, luminous eyes. And I was cursing to myself. These days a man never got anywhere because of intruders! There ought to be a law against it, I thought savagely, and then that knocking on the door became a ferocious pounding with fists that must have contained a lot of beef.

# 7

### Khilil's a--!

I sat up, growling savagely to myself, 'Who in heck's name is out there?'

Had someone after all seen me enter this room and then come up to dig me out? I thought if that was so then there would be other monkeys standing below this fire escape and I'd be trapped.

A sudden thought occurred to me. For the first time I spoke to that Rumanian girl. She was sitting up now, and hugging close to me as if she was afraid — and afraid for my safety, I thought. I liked her for that.

I said, 'That gun?' I was remembering the automatic that had been knocked to the floor in the ruckus with the two monkeys who had surprised me in this apartment the day previously.

She said, 'The police took it with them.'

So that was no good. Whoever was trying to smash that door in wouldn't find me armed when they trampled over the splintered ruins.

Then the pounding ceased, and I heard a voice raised in high, angry tones out in that corridor. I listened incredulously.

It was B.G.'s voice!

I turned and looked at that Rumanian and I couldn't believe my ears. Why was inhibited B.G. wanting to bust his way into the Rumanian's apartment at this time of night?

She must have realised what I was thinking, for she shook her head slowly, and I knew she was as mystified as I was.

Then I began to distinguish words in B.G.'s loud speech. I also tumbled to something else, too.

B.G. was a very drunken man.

I got it then. Those bright boys, Marty, Dwight, Harry Sauer and the others must have found time heavy on their hands, and this night they'd got B.G. drunk instead of little Miss Dunkley. And the drink had brought out the animal in B.G. — he'd lost his inhibitions.

Now I could hear him out there in the passage, roaring for little Lavinia. By God, he was going to show her, he was telling the world!

I could imagine the boys standing along that corridor, gleefully listening and watching the big fat slob make a fool of himself. It would do him good, anyway.

Then someone must have told him he was at the wrong door. I heard him go and thump on a door up the corridor, and it sounded to be the next one to the Rumanian's. He didn't thump long.

We sat there on that bed together for minutes afterwards, listening — and hearing nothing more.

At length I sighed and drew her to me. Now her shoulders were cold because they had been exposed. I got my arms round her and pressed her to me, and I soon put the warmth back in them. Her lips were brushing mine, and I could hear her murmuring, 'It was good of you to remember me in your trouble. I will be able to repay you because I think I can get a job. The Gazino — '

But I wasn't interested in the Gazino

and a job as entertainer there.

It was still dark when I went back to my apartment under the roof of the Armenian's dwelling. I didn't want to leave that hot-blooded Rumanian, but there was no future in staying in her apartment. I had to be down by that square for when Yusef Khilil put on his act.

Time passed — pleasantly. At length, I took another shower because I didn't know when I'd get my next one, and then said goodbye and went down the fire escape. This time I had no adventures on my way to my temporary abode.

When I reached it I found myself a tired man. I climbed into bed, and the parcel I had brought with me I dropped on the floor close to my hand.

That parcel had caused the Rumanian to be very suspicious and even indignant, but I had used my Heggy charm to soothe her down, and she had given me what I had asked for.

I'd made promises to Baby, and I mightn't live long and I wanted to fulfil those promises.

In that parcel were those nylon

171

undergarments that I had promised smiling, peasant-faced Baby. They were the Rumanian's, but from what I'd seen of her wardrobe she wouldn't miss them.

I came out of a beautiful sleep in which I thought I was back in the warm embrace of my Rumanian again.

Instead I opened my eyes on Baby's happy, smiling features. She had brought me my breakfast.

I sat up, grinning. The Armenian was there, looking very depressed. Baby looked at him as if she wished he wasn't there, but she said nothing. I picked up the parcel and tossed it across to Baby, who caught it eagerly. She was guessing what was inside.

Her fingers trembled as she pulled open one end so that she could see for herself what the paper contained. She pulled out some white undergarments, and her eyes widened and then she started to croon as she saw the black rose that had been worked in by the left leg. She played with the garments as if they were living things. And she was in ecstasy.

She went away at length. Next time she

came back she was wearing all her finery under that tattered dress. I knew it because of the exquisite happiness on that simple, merry face of hers. She had her shoes on, and they were killing her, but she was bearing the pain with fortitude. Her nylons were slimming her mighty legs and making them look attractive. And through that rent in her dress, I saw the whiteness of a garment probably unusual to her. She was a happy girl.

The Armenian was there again. I was keeping him there, because I didn't want any complications with Baby.

The Armenian wasn't feeling good this morning. He'd taken round his Youth Restorer the previous night, and he'd got so enthusiastic about it that he had drunk several bottles himself. The raw alcohol had left him with hammers hitting him on the skull this morning, and he was inclined to be pessimistic about the benefits of feeling young again.

Especially he was pessimistic about the meeting that night. Time after time his lugubrious voice, so unlike its usual pleasant self, said, 'They will kill you.

When they see you they won't let you speak. They'll all come forward and they'll tear the flesh off your bones.'

The way he said it he seemed to take some enjoyment at the thought. I told him to quit beefing and told him I could do what I liked with the flesh on my bones, couldn't I?

We weren't good company for each other, but we sat and played backgammon during the hot afternoon, and listened to the hum of traffic below and the cries of street pedlars.

But then night came, and we looked down and realised that the meeting was beginning. There was a crowd already beginning to gather. And as the minutes passed it grew thicker and thicker until finally all traffic was stopped and then all at once it seemed that that square below had become packed solid with humanity. The big U.N.P. meeting had begun.

One car was allowed to crawl right into the middle, and it looked to be Mustapha Agloul's car, and then I saw the murderer himself get up and begin a harangue of the crowd.

Little did he know why his second-in-command, Yusef Khilil, had organised this meeting that night!

I looked down upon the scene, upon the heads of thousands of people, showing as a blurred and shadowy mass in the darkness below, a darkness relieved only by the glaring lights from sidewalk cafés that ringed the square.

Mustapha, revealed plainly up there on top of that sedan, talked a long time. He talked in the strident tones of a soapbox orator, a true demagogue. His voice was coarse and kept rising in waves of anger that affected his audience similarly. As time went on almost every sentence that he shouted was greeted with a savage, raw-throated response from the mob. Even without understanding a word of Turkish I knew that he was inciting them, whipping them into a fury of madness that would make them do as he wanted . . . and he wanted them to do something bad this night.

When I asked the Armenian, 'What's that guy beefing about?' he just shrugged.

'The same old stuff.'

'Turkey for the Turks? Throw out the damned foreigner who is getting a hold on his country, huh?'

He nodded. It was the old stuff. Half those people down below lived better because the United Nations were pumping money into a country so poor that most of its people hardly ever tasted meat more than a couple of times a year.

I said, 'A crowd's a sucker for any spiel from a politician,' but I was getting uneasy.

Where was Yusef Khilil?

I kept watching for him and he never showed up. Then the Armenian began to be nervous, too, and he said, 'Mustapha Agloul wants them to go and set fire to the American hotel. He wants to precipitate a crisis, as he says.'

The crowd, inflamed by what they believed to be true, that Habib Pasha had been removed by an American because of his nationalist beliefs, were roaring approval of the incendiary talk . . .

We heard the telephone ringing in the Armenian's room. He went out quickly, leaving me in a room that was again filled with moonlight. I watched and waited, and I was praying now to see Yusef Khilil appear and upset all Mustapha Agloul's plans. I listened to the ranting voice of the mob leader, and I saw the swaying movement from the crowd below that told of the effect of his words.

Someone came in behind me. I heard the door close softly. I wheeled, crouching instantly at the thought of danger. It was the Armenian. He had a bottle of his Youth Restorer in his hand, and by the look of it he had been drinking heavily in the minutes that he had been absent.

I stared at him. He swilled liquid down his throat, and his eyes were apprehensive. He didn't move away from the door.

I said, 'It's bad news.' I didn't even put a question mark at the end of my sentence. I knew it was.

The Armenian nodded. He said, 'That was Yusef Khilil.'

I didn't have to be told. I said, 'He's gone yellow, huh? He daren't face Mustapha. He's a — '

I went on for a long time saying what kind of a man Yusef Khilil was, but it didn't do any good. It just meant that I had inspired more trouble by getting Yusef to plan this meeting below my window. It didn't bring me any nearer salvation for myself.

The Armenian got his mouth away from that bottle and then said, 'You'd better get out of here quickly. I think Yusef will play double and try to get you handed over to Mustapha Agloul's supporters.'

It was the sort of thing Mustapha would do. He'd try to exterminate me if only to keep my mouth shut. I started to go out of that room which was no longer a refuge for me — started to go down the stairs that terminated right on the backs of that frenzied mob that was screaming for the life of Joe P. Heggy.

# 8

## Bomb in a bottle

When I was at the head of that staircase I turned and looked back along the moonlit passage and I saw the Armenian standing in the doorway of the room I had just quit. He was holding an empty bottle by his side. He said, 'I'm sorry.'

I reckon he was sorry, too. He was a rascal, but there was a lot that was likeable about the crimp-haired Armenian.

I nodded. I said, 'Where was Yusef when he phoned you?'

But that Armenian didn't hear me. He'd gone into his own room and there was a bit of a stagger about his gait. The Youth Restorer sure had a kick in it to produce such an effect in such a short time.

I waited. He came out of his room and he was carrying one of his precious bottles of liquor. I was touched. It was a demonstration of friendship. He shoved the bottle into my hand.

'When you feel bad, drink. It is good.' He looked cock-eyed at me and I had to put that bottle into my pocket. I couldn't offend him.

Then I repeated my question. The Armenian said, 'He was at the U.N.P. headquarters.' Then his head lifted sharply and he came out of the drunken glaze that had begun to film his eyes. He said, quickly, 'You're not thinking of going there, Mr. Heggy?'

There was real concern in his voice. I clumped him on the shoulder and said. 'Maybe. You keep watch from the window. Maybe you'll see something.' And then I started to go down those dirty worn wooden steps.

I wasn't through yet! The hell with it, I was saying, I might as well be hanged for a sheep as a lamb. There was just a chance I might save the situation yet — though it was a slim chance.

But I had to get out of that building and then get away from that crowded square without being detected I was on the second flight down when I thought my chances were already ruined . . .

Someone was coming slowly, painfully up those stairs. Even then I got the impression that it was a painful ascent, that someone was crawling up the steps.

I got on to a landing and stood back against the wall and hoped that the moonlight that lit this passage wouldn't reveal me — but I was sure it would — moonlight shows up pretty well.

I saw someone creeping into view up the stairway. I was crouched ready to jump, my fists bunched ready to hit out. I was a desperate man. I wasn't going to have the name 'Heggy' shouted out to bring that mob storming to get me and lynch me. No man goes out without a fight.

Then my fists slowly opened. I saw something brown and pleasant and knew there was no danger for me. I relaxed and moved towards the head of those stairs.

I bent and put my hands under mighty arms and hoisted.

Baby came up in confusion. Yet she was

grinning like the big-hearted girl she was. She was in her finery again and those shoes were killing her. But a gal suffers a lot in the interests of fashion.

She stood there and grinned and giggled and then made motions towards her mouth. She had come to see if I wanted anything to eat and drink. She sure looked after me, that mighty Amazon,

I shook my head. I was thinking rapidly. Baby could be a very useful ally if only I could get past this crowd.

I pointed down the steps. I said a perfectly good Turkish word and she understood it. It was, 'Taksi.'

She said, 'Taksi,' and nodded understandingly and started to go down those steps to get me one. I followed.

It wasn't a pleasant feeling, going out onto that crowded square. To get out of the crowd we had to shove our way behind their backs. If any one had turned and recognised me, with the occasional light showing my American suiting — so unmistakably American — I wouldn't have lived more than a second.

But Mustapha was going to town up

there on that sedan over the heads of the mob, and what he was saying was appealing to their frustrated, overworked, undernourished souls. They had ears for only Mustapha and eyes for no one else. Baby came in useful. She just bundled her way round the rear of the crowd, and I followed on her heels. She had taken off her shoes, and was padding along in nylons that had begun to fall down over her knees.

We came to an alley and Baby went into it. It was very dark, and I kept close behind Baby in case I lost her.

Then again we found ourselves in an open space where trolley cars ran. Baby looked back at me. There was a taxi right ahead. I called to Baby, 'U.N.P.' She understood those three initials. And she guessed the rest. She had quite a bit of shrewdness behind that peasant face of hers.

She went back to the taxi driver and while she was chattering to him, I slipped into the back of his taxi from the opposite side. I didn't want any taxi-driver to spot me just yet.

Baby got in beside me. She was giggling non-stop now, and I guessed this was the first time in her life she had ever ridden in a taxi. The occasion was so great that she even started to put her shoes on again, and then she must have guessed there was work for her to do at the other end, and she removed them, and then carefully removed her stockings again.

I could feel the mighty muscles of her thigh as she contorted in the back of the taxi to get her nylons off without making holes in them.

All the way across that familiar iron bridge and up the steep trolley track beyond, I was praying for Mustapha to keep on talking. If once he stopped and a procession formed up, then there'd be no stopping the crowd in what they were setting out to do.

I wanted to get Yusef and drag him down there and shove him up on that sedan and make him talk.

And I figured that if I could do all that before the crowd started to march, then I reckoned I stood a chance of turning that crowd against their treacherous new leader, Mustapha Agloul.

It was a desperate throw, and only a man in a desperate condition would have entertained the idea.

I knew that car driver was racing faster than was safe, but all Istanbul taxi drivers do that. But still it didn't seem to be going half fast enough.

I was in a fever as I watched the buildings flit by on either side of us. I wanted to be there already, and I was thumping my knees and cursing the driver because he couldn't fly.

Baby got a bit amorous towards the end of our trip, no doubt affected by this taxi ride in the same way that the Armenian's Youth Restorer affected whim. But I let it all pass. I kept my mind on my business, and my business right then was trying to save the Heggy neck.

The taxi pulled up outside the approach to the U.N.P. headquarters. There was a long passage that came off the main road, like the one I'd run up the previous night, and then there was an open space and this old Turkish building, with its overhanging bay windows that had been made into a political party's headquarters.

I got out. The taxi-driver saw me and looked startled. Then Baby padded after me and we were lost in the shadows. The taxi-driver sat there and waited. He hadn't been paid, so he had to wait. He must have figured that he hadn't seen right, because no American would surely walk into the U.N.P.'s headquarters like I was doing.

I didn't walk into that lighted building. When we were down the passageway and just entering onto that open court-yard, I halted in the shadows. I looked up at those yellow, lighted windows and saw occasional figures moving about within the building.

I thought there wouldn't be many here tonight, because most of the party workers would be down organising that demonstration in the square. That was in my favour.

I caught hold of Baby's mighty bicep and told her, 'Fetch Yusef Khilil to me.'

The only words she'd understand were

Yusef Khilil, but she cottoned on, I could see, right away.

She pointed to where I was standing and she nodded and went padding off into the building, leaving me to hold her shoes and nylons. I waited several minutes, so long that I began to think that things had gone wrong.

Then I heard a man's voice and recognised it as Yusef Khilil's . . .

I was suddenly tickled to death. I could look through the open doorway into the broad high hall that is the central feature of all these old Turkish houses. It was lit by a solitary naked electric lamp that surged in intensity with current fluctuations.

I saw Yusef Khilil appear in the hallway, and he was talking loudly and protesting. He was trying to turn to argue, but every time he tried to stop, Baby just walked into him and shoved him with her stomach. Baby's stomach was too much for a simple politician. He found himself being bundled towards the doorway by a big, grinning, ragged-dressed Turkish girl, and he had to go whether he wanted to or not.

He didn't want to and that was why he was arguing.

I saw some men appear at the end of the hallway, and they were staring in astonishment at the party's No. 2 being treated in that manner. I saw them look at each other and talk quickly, and I knew they were asking, 'What do we do about this?'

But Baby got Yusef outside and down those steps before they had made up their minds. And then he was being shoved on her navel across to where I stood in the darkness.

I gave her back her shoes and nylons and then I took that treacherous politician by the shirt neck and I started to twist it until it must have hurt. He looked at me like a tortoise, with his head curiously recessed into his shoulders. His eyes were protruding more than ever, and his nose was long and craggy and did look like a tortoise's. I said, 'I hate to do this to you, Yusef, but I figure on living a bit longer. You said you would talk to the crowd and tell them the truth about Mustapha Agloul.'

He tried to get enough air through his throat to speak to me. He said, 'I didn't dare. They might have turned on me before I could have said more than one sentence.'

I was looking beyond him now, to where a group of men were standing in the doorway. They must have seen me in the shadows, and were recognising that I wasn't doing their No. 2 any good.

I said, 'Yusef, you're coming with me. You're going up there beside Mustapha and you're going to tell the crowd everything just as we planned.' Then I added to the argument. 'If you don't, I'm going to hand myself over to the police and I'm going to tell them a story.'

He said quickly, 'A story?'

'Yeah. That story will indict you, brother. I shall tell them you knew who was the killer of Habib Pasha, but you hadn't the guts to speak out about it. I'll tell them something else, too, and that is that you were prepared to take money from an American corporation, for your own pocket!'

That got him on the raw. Suddenly he

was so agitated that he nearly strangled himself in my grasp.

Suddenly he realised the consequences of that little conversation with me.

He started to deny it. 'I never meant it. I shall say so.'

I shook my head sadly. 'They won't believe you. They never believe a politician when someone says they talked graft to them.'

Those boys were coming across from the lighted doorway now. I think they were beginning to see that this man who was gripping their No. 2 so painfully was no Turk. Then I heard an incredulous gasp and then I knew that if I hadn't been recognised, they at least saw that I was an American.

I swung Yusef round and started to shove him down the alley. He was protesting. Fear of being torn to pieces by his own mob was stronger at that moment than the fear of being exposed as a half-hearted grafter.

I bundled him down that alleyway. He was going the way I wanted, and he was going to stand up there and talk to that crowd — even if it killed him!

Baby was padding on ahead, scared. Behind us half a dozen Turks of the U.N.P. were starting to come into the alley. They were shouting, too, and their manner was very threatening.

I hadn't a weapon of any sort . . .

I held Yusef by the neck with one hand, pulled out that bottle that a grateful Armenian had given me. The light shone upon the black object. I stood there in the attitude of a man about to throw something, and I said to Yusef, 'I'll blow us all up with this bomb if they come a step nearer.'

Yusef believed it. Yusef's voice lifted in panic and he shouted agitatedly to the following Turks to stay where they were. This was a bomb, he must have told them.

They halted so suddenly they seemed to have grown roots. I bundled Yusef backwards down that alley until we came to the taxi. Then I slung Yusef into the rear. The taxi-driver half-rose from his seat, because he didn't understand what it was all about. I shoved some money into his hand and that did a lot of explaining. Anyway, it told him who was master of this situation. Me, the man with plenty of jack.

Baby got in, then, and the taxi started to move away though I hadn't told him my destination.

I told Yusef, 'You tell him to take us to the square where the meeting is.'

Yusef seemed suddenly to become resigned, though he had a hunted look about him. He shouted through the window to the taxi-driver.

I said, 'You tell him to go faster than he's ever gone before, and tell him there's plenty dough coming if we get there quickly and in one piece.'

Asking a taxi-driver in Istanbul to go fast is asking for a quick death, but this one was charmed. Other people suffered down that winding, cobble-stoned trolley track, but we got through unscathed.

All the way down I gave Yusef a pep talk. I had started by threatening him, and he knew I would carry out my threats. Now I told him of the glories of party leadership that were within his grasp if only he had the guts to reach out and take them for himself.

'I reckon you'll be the No. 1 politician in all Turkey within a few years,' I told him. 'If you're not the premier, you'll at least be a very, very wealthy man. I'll see to that. You keep control of your party, and I'll see you get a cut in any contract we get here in your country.'

It was dirty talk, but I was only looking after myself; for the first thing was to get Mustapha Agloul labelled for the killer he was.

By the time we got to that square Yusef was so bursting with determination to oust Mustapha Agloul that I felt sure he would go through with the plan as we had first arranged it. When we got to the meeting, I breathed a sigh of thankfulness. Mustapha Agloul loved the sound of his own voice, and it was proving his own undoing. He was still talking, hating the moment when he would have to stop. The procession — the demonstration that was to end with the burning of the American's hotel — was still being talked about and hadn't begun.

I shoved Yusef out of the taxi. I paid the taxi-driver so much it never occurred to him to shout and tell those back-turned Turks that here was an American right within their reach.

Baby scuttled off into the darkness with her shoes and nylons.

Yusef began to push his way through the crowd, shouting his name as he did so, and they parted to let him go through, and patted him on the back and tried to shake his hand as demonstrative Turks always do when in the presence of the great.

I walked right through that crowd, right on the heels of the smaller, strutting Yusef, and they never saw me. They were watching Yusef, and couldn't see me, a tall man behind the politician, in that bad light.

Up on the sedan Mustapha Agloul looked down at the commotion and saw Yusef Khilil coming towards him. He smiled a false smile and held out his arms as if he loved this man — and he didn't know what a serpent he was preparing to embrace.

I kept my gaze fixed all the time upon the squat-headed Yusef. I was watching him for treachery.

Yet he must have seen in that moment his grand opportunity, and he was prepared to take the risks now. Power-dazzled, Yusef was blinded by the possibilities of the situation, even though before he had weighed the chances of success and been unimpressed by the margin in his favour.

Mustapha reached down from the sedan and pulled his comrade up beside him. Then they stood together, with Mustapha's arm around the more stunted Yusef's shoulders, and Mustapha shouted to the crowd as if inviting applause for one of their leaders. He got it. A crowd will applaud anything.

I stood there, anonymous in the darkness of that crowd, a crowd that pressed so tightly against me that.

I could feel the hardness of that Youth Restorer in my pocket. I wished I'd got rid of it earlier. It had had its moment of usefulness, and now at times it quite hurt as the crowd swayed and I took the pressure on my thigh. But the crowd was too thick for me to pull out that bottle and dispose of it.

I was watching Yusef. He had moved away from under the protective arm of his No. 1. Now his hands were raised for silence, and Mustapha, genial in his success, arrogantly generous because he was top dog, waved his arms and shouted to the crowd to give ear to Yusef. I thought grimly: He wouldn't be doing that if he knew what was coming!

I didn't know what was said, but I didn't need an interpreter. I could guess what Yusef was saying.

He started to speak, and his voice was high-pitched and rattled words out as if he were afraid he would be stopped before he had said his piece. The murmuring of the crowd ceased almost with his first word. I realised that everyone around me was rigid in their attention upon the orator.

I looked up at Mustapha Agloul's face, as he stood on the roof of that big sedan. It was incredulous. He couldn't believe what he was hearing. For a few seconds he stood there irresolute, not knowing what to do to silence this man whom he had just greeted as a friend.

In that time the damage was done, I guess. Yusef fired words over the heads of the crowd, and they sank in, He was telling them, I guessed, that there had been bad blood between Habib Pasha and Mustapha Agloul. That Mustapha was due to be purged. Instead, Mustapha had eliminated their beloved leader.

Of course he would be their beloved leader. Always a dead politician is beloved by everyone especially by the men who hope to succeed him.

The crowd suddenly gasped, and I knew then that Yusef, pointing at the goggle-eyed Mustapha, was saying that here was the killer, that here was the man who had treacherously slipped a knife into Habib's back and then tried to put the blame on someone else.

Mustapha suddenly seemed to scream with rage.

It was a noise I'd once heard from a maddened horse on a racetrack. It wasn't a nice kind of sound, but then Mustapha wasn't a nice kind of guy. His arms flailed, and then started to beat upon the head of Yusef Khilil. A curious grim humour came to me then, that maybe Yusef had been thumped a lot on his head in his political career, which accounted for its being somehow recessed into his shoulders.

They were standing together on that sedan, fighting like school kids — feminine variety. They hadn't any idea of smacking out with their fists and they were just pulling and screaming at each other and trying not to fall off the sedan.

The crowd woke up. I got the impression immediately that some believed Yusef and others denied it. They were beginning to brawl among themselves, and then all in an instant it seemed as though fighting spread out right throughout that square. I found myself suddenly swept up to that sedan.

I thought I'd go up and try to help Yusef. He'd done his bit, now I must do mine.

But I hadn't reckoned on addressing an audience that was madly trying to tear the guts out of each other.

I climbed on to the sedan. Mustapha saw me coming, and I saw his big, sallow face crack open with surprise when he recognised me. He must have guessed who I was because I looked so obviously American.

The crowd stopped fighting when they saw me. Instead a good half of them tried to get at me and pull me down and tear me into small, raw pieces.

I held up my hands for silence. I got it. Perhaps it was my effrontery in facing them openly that won me a hearing. But they gave it to me.

I looked down upon faces that were lined and hard and sallow, and mostly stubble-bearded. These were the poorer elements of Istanbul's population — the men who got least out of life and were ready to back a cause that said they could get more. And yet they were willing to listen to me.

They didn't understand a word I said, but there was Yusef to interpret, sentence by sentence, as I spoke.

I shouted, 'It is as Yusef Khilil says. Mustapha Agloul killed Habib Pasha. I saw it happen. I was on an aircraft and I saw the killing take place only a few feet below me as we came in to land.'

'I didn't kill Habib. I couldn't have done. I was in that aircraft, and the police will already have checked with the passengers and found that I did in fact report the killing in that plane before we landed.'

'I tell you, Mustapha Agloul's a no-good, two-timing murderer. You want to have nothing to do with him. You'll find Yusef Khilil is a better man!'

I could say that and believe it. It still didn't say much for Yusef Khilil — only that so far, to my knowledge, he hadn't killed anyone to further his cause.

I'd been keeping my eyes open while I was talking, and I'd seen how men were wriggling their way through the crowd all the time I spoke, heading for that car on which Mustapha Agloul was standing with us. When I'd finished my little spiel, I saw Mustapha suddenly jump down from the sedan, and I realised that he had jumped into the arms of his musclemen. They'd come trekking through that crowd towards their leader, and now he was safe in their midst.

But I wasn't safe. While Yusef was still translating my speech to a crowd that roared savagely with every statement he made, I saw that tough-faced mob of Turkish musclemen begin to swarm round the sedan. They were going to stop Yusef from finishing my speech, and the way their eyes looked up at me I knew they were going to stop me forever.

Just for one moment I didn't know what to do. It wasn't much good turning that crowd in Yusef's favour if neither of us got out of the shindig alive.

Then I felt that weight in my pocket again, and I blessed the Armenian — that little drunk who was no doubt at this moment staring down upon the crowded scene in the square below him.

I pulled out that flat, flask-like bottle of black liquid. My thumb cupped over the squat neck and then it could look like anything,

I swung it aloft, and I shouted, 'If anyone tries to get me, we'll all go up in smoke!'

The thing was, Yusef still believed it was a bomb himself. Suddenly he stopped translating my earlier speech, and I heard him scream frantically and point to the object in my hand, and I knew he was saying it was a bomb and I was crazy enough to use it. Yusef was sweating pounds away at that moment, because he didn't want to go out on the blast of a bomb at the height of his political career.

Neither did those bozos below. They halted where they were in the act of climbing on to the sedan all around me. I made a threatening gesture as if to hurl the bomb down into their midst, and I saw their eyes widen and their faces go a sickly colour.

Then they let go of the car and started to press back into the crowd. In a matter of seconds it was astonishing bow much clear space there was around that sedan.

Yusef was kneeling on the sedan now, as if about to tumble off the car himself. He was looking up at me, and he looked pitiful.

I told him to get up and make the most of this opportunity. I told him to demand that the crowd take Mnstapha Agloul and hand him over to the police on a charge of murder, and that I would bear witness against him.

Yusef got to his feet and was in his stride in a moment — vocally speaking. His finger was stabbing out to where Mustapha Agloul stood among his supporters. His voice chattered like a machine-gun, spitting words against his No. 1.

That crowd reacted to a positive suggestion of action. Those who believed Yusef — and me — surged forward to take Mustapha — probably not to take him to any police station, but to effect justice on him in the way of mobs.

But Mustapha was a politician and had many of that crowd in his pocket, and they had supporters. It became a pitched battle again, down there in the square.

Fascinated I looked down upon a scene of turmoil such as I've never witnessed before. Several thousand people were hitting out at each other, clawing and scratching and kicking, and every one of them screaming hate at the top of his voice.

Yusef grabbed me by the arm in alarm.

He shouted something in Turkish, he was so agitated.

I understood, though not from his words. Mustapha Agloul's strong-arm boys were pressing back towards the car now, and in a moment it looked as though we would be surrounded.

I jumped to the ground. Yusef rolled down after me, and we retired to where we thought we had supporters. Some of them weren't. I had to hit a couple of them to make them realise that I wasn't standing for being mauled by Mustapha's men.

We did find ourselves in a group of supporters, and then we found ourselves like an island surrounded by Mustapha's men. We had the damnedest battle in that square, striking out all the time at enemies. I'd shoved that bottle back into my pocket, because it seemed useless as a threat at close quarters where the label on it might be seen.

A big, dirty ruffian came lurching at me suddenly. I knocked him on to his knees with a blow to his jaw that jarred me right up to my elbow. I saw his mouth open with pain, a mouth without many teeth that looked ugly in its surround of many days' growth of beard.

Then that big Turk seemed to fall against me, and his hand ripped and a pocket tore. I got back quickly, because he had strength and I didn't want to get into any close fighting with him.

I saw him holding something, on his knees and resting on one hand. I realised that that bottle had come out with my pocket, and he was staring at it stupidly, perhaps reading the label and guessing what manner of 'bomb' had deterred him and his friends.

Youth Restorer!

We fought back then, and went on the retreat. It wasn't as if Mustapha had more supporters than Yusef; it was just that Yusef and I were the target for all Mustapha's men and we had no option but to go fighting and retreating all the time.

I found myself with my back brushing against a wall, and I realised that a surging movement of that vast, fighting crowd had swept us right up against a building that bordered the square. It gave me an idea. Joe P. Heggy thought there were quite enough people fighting without him being there. Besides, inevitably in the end someone was going to do Joe P. Heggy no good at all. It was that kind of a brawl.

I started to fight my way along the edge of the crowd, and then I saw a familiar doorway. There was a swirl of bodies around me and I ducked inside, and I was sure no one noticed the way I'd gone.

I went up those worn, dirty wooden stairs, and came out on to a moonlit landing. I walked the length of the passage and then started to climb the next staircase. Halfway up I paused to listen. There was not a sound from the staircase, though plenty from the square outside. No one was following me.

I gave a sigh of relief and straightened my clothes, which had suffered considerably in the fighting. Then I started to climb those stairs right to the top landing, where a drunken Armenian would still be an ally . . .

I saw bare feet right in front of my nose. Mighty feet. Then I realised there was a sheen upon them, and knew them to be nylon-covered.

I lifted my eyes and there was Baby sitting on the top step in the shadows. I halted and looked at her.

She was smiling at me, in that big, friendly way of hers. I grinned back. It was like a meeting of old friends.

Her shoes were at her side. She was like any other Western woman who took off her shoes to rest her aching dogs. She just sat and smiled at me.

I'd come up here to do things, and I was going to do them. Baby wasn't on the itinerary — yet.

I said, 'You need a new dress, honey. Okay, I'll fix you in a good one first thing tomorrow.'

Because I had a feeling that after all Joe P. Heggy was going to circulate in Istanbul for quite a time now.

She was sharp and she got on to my promise right away. Her face lifted eagerly and she said, 'Nylon?' — the only word of English she knew.

I nodded. 'A nylon dress for Baby,' I promised.

Then I walked past her, patting her black, coarse hair as I did so. I left her in ecstasy, thinking of the nylon dress that would complete the rest of the nylon outfit that this wonderful American had brought into her peasant life.

I opened the Armenian's bottle-filled room. It was full of full bottles, but no Armenian.

I tramped on to the room I'd occupied looking over the front of the building, and found the Armenian draped over the windowsill, watching the packed square intent on exterminating itself eighty feet below.

I looked round. My room was full of empty bottles.

The Armenian had been going to town on his stock during my absence. I levered him off the window ledge, and I saw that he was very, very drunk. He recognised me, and hiccupped in my face. The stink of aniseed was appalling. I said to him, 'You've got to get me some numbers on that telephone. Sober up, fellow, will ya?'

I got him down to his room. Where Baby sat.

I paused and listened. There was no sound on the stairs. Now I was completely reassured. Now I knew that no one had seen my departure.

I shoved the Armenian into his crowded room.

He tried to grab for another bottle, and clawed air two feet short of it. He was that bad.

I shoved the telephone into his hand and told him to get me George, the police officer whom I knew.

In a moment of inspiration I was able to remember George's real name and rank. It was the first time I'd ever done it. George didn't have the kind of name a westerner can easily remember.

Somehow the Armenian got me through. Probably the telephone exchange reacted more promptly when it was a call for the police.

I introduced myself. I heard that young police officer's voice, and it sounded pleasantly amused, as if the antics of the Americans were something faintly comical. He asked, 'When are you coming to give yourself up? You know we only want to get you out of this country for your own sake.'

I said, 'You can come and get me right away, though I don't think you'll need to shove me out of the country. I've just split a political party.'

By the sounds outside the split was going to be something that wouldn't be healed quickly. I didn't tell the police officer that if Yusef's side won, which I anticipated, I would have him in my pocket, anyway.

I said, 'You should get your men down here right away. And have them watch out for the new U.N.P. leader, Mustapha Agloul. I'm telling you he's the man that killed Habib Pasha.'

There was silence from the other end of the wire. I had expected surprise again I was disappointed. I had a feeling that no one was surprised at anything Mustapha Agloul might have done.

So I went on, 'I'm prepared to give evidence that I saw Mustapha Agloul slip a knife into Habib Pasha's back. I've just publicly announced that fact to his supporters, and they're fighting among themselves now,'

He told me to wait where I was, and I gave him my address and said I'd wait. There was nothing more I could do now.

While I was waiting I thought I'd ring B.G. and tell him the good news. The Armenian detached himself from a bottle and got me the number. It was the last thing he did that day. He passed out with his next gulp of Youth Restorer.

B.G. came on to the phone, querulous and unhappy. I told him he could quit worrying.

'The boys will be back on the site tomorrow, B.G. I've split the U.N.P. It doesn't count any more.'

I thought I'd hear B.G. cheer at that, but he just said nothing. I waited a few seconds, then asked sharply, 'Aren't you glad?'

He seemed to jerk his thoughts back to the job in hand. Vaguely he said, 'Yeah, sure I'm glad, Joe. You're a regular trouble-buster, aren't you?'

I said, modestly, 'That's my job, B.G.'

I waited for more bouquets, and none came. So I got mighty mad and I bellowed, 'Is that all you've got to say to me? The hell, I risked my life to sort this problem out, and you just say I'm a nice little boy.'

B.G.'s voice came wearily over the wire to me. 'I reckon I'm not myself today. I — I feel . . . bad.'

I had a sudden mental picture of B.G. slumped in a chair, his face grey behind those prissy, business-tycoon's glasses of his. And I suddenly guessed why.

I said, softly, 'I figure you've spent your life's savings, huh?'

B.G. said, 'What?' — not understanding.

So I told him. 'All these years, B.G., you've been saving yourself up for the right woman. And last night — '

There was a yelp of alarm from him. 'How do you know?' It must have amazed him, for he couldn't have suspected that I'd been in the Rumanian's room during his drunken outburst.

I told him it was a little bird, and he said, 'The hell with the little bird. Does everybody know?'

I said, innocently, 'Know what?'

He groaned. He was a man in torment. He said, 'I feel defiled. The boys got me drunk last night, and honest to God, I didn't know what I was doing. I went in to that little Englishwoman.'

I thought I heard the door handle behind me. Baby was probably bringing coffee in. Baby was always bringing coffee in.

I said, bluntly, 'What's wrong with you, B.G., is that you're suffering from a hangover. It's alcoholic remorse, not anything else.'

I thought: I'll bet Lavinia isn't feeling bad this morning.

Lavinia, late in her life, had tumbled to a few truths, and now she was making up for lost time. She wouldn't be pretending otherwise.

I felt a draught. I started to turn, the phone clutched to my ear. The Armenian was snoring noisily, slumped in a chair with a broken straw bottom.

The door swung back with a bang on its hinges.

A lot of men stood in that doorway. An awful lot.

I stood up. They weren't moving, they were so sure they had me.

I said, 'B.G. I'm ringing off. Friends have just dropped in.'

One of them stepped forward. His face looked as if it had been recently knocked about a bit. There was an ugly stubble around an even uglier mouth. I thought back to when I had last seen that face. It had been clutching a torn pocket and a bottle that had gone with that torn pocket.

I looked at bony shafts of arms that ended in big bony hands and in those hands was clutched . . . a Youth Restorer bottle.

I thought, resignedly: Sure, I got into this place unseen.

But I'd left the address in that Mustapha Agloul's supporter's hands.

# 9

. . . a girl like that

I picked up a bottle of Youth Restorer and laid one of them out first clout.

The room began to shake to the tread of their feet as they jumped at me. There were about five of them, and that looked an awful lot of humanity in that overcrowded room.

I jumped straight to meet them, because there was no sense in going back, and I picked a sore jaw and smacked it again with every ounce of strength I had. I was doing well. The bozo went into a corner, writhing in agony. Two clumps on the jaw within the space of a quarter of an hour was more than was good for a man.

Then I realised that Mustapha Agloul was one of the men himself. He'd got his knife out. Evidently he habitually toted a knife.

He was the danger man to watch.

It was the goldarndest ruckus I've ever been in. You can't put several fighting men in one small, overcrowded room and not reduce it to shambles within seconds.

One of the Turks cracked me on the cheekbone and sent me crashing into the Armenian's stacks of bottles. The whole lot came down with a rumbling roar, and after that we fought on rolling bottles.

They showered over my head and shoulders as I fell against the piled boxes, and I saw them fall on to the Armenian who'd got tipped out of his chair.

Some of the bottles became unstoppered and liquid flowed close by his head.

I saw his eyes open dazedly, his tongue licked gratefully, and then he passed out again.

I was fighting with feet and fists, trying to keep Mustapha Agloul away with his knife. Every time I could I picked up a bottle and hurled it at my opponents, and when they crashed against the wall they exploded like bombs.

There was liquor and broken glass everywhere.

Over it all we fought. The guy with the

sore jaw was back in the fight now, and I'd four men against me. I kept trying to hook that sore jaw, but he kept it just out of reach.

They were going to town with their fists and feet on me, and I was a raging mass of pain within minutes,

But never once did Mustapha get near me with that wicked knife of his. I just managed to evade each lunge as he came for me. The fact that so many men were in that room was in some way an asset to me — they kept getting in Mustapha's way.

Then I saw a wonderful sight. There was Baby standing in the doorway, a mighty figure of a woman in her torn dress and glamorous nylons.

She was looking with indignation that changed to anger at those men who attacked me. Almost I could hear her saying, 'If he goes, bang goes my chance of getting a nylon dress!'

Baby reacted instantly to that thought. She scooped up an opponent and I saw her wheel with him in her mighty arms, and then she dropped him down the stairs. The way she dropped him I figured he wouldn't be back in the fight for minutes.

Then Baby turned to come back and do the same again, and I was rooting for the gal.

But someone kicked on the door and it slammed in her face, and some sort of catch dropped which wasn't operated from outside. Or maybe the lock functioned automatically, though they don't usually in Turkey.

It shut out my powerful ally, and I was trapped inside that room with three men who wanted my life.

There was no doubt about their intentions. They wanted to eliminate me, because I was the witness who could incriminate Mustapha Agloul. With me out of the way he had nothing to fear, because there wouldn't be an eyewitness of his misdeed.

I knew it and I fought with everything I'd got, and I cursed the Armenian who was lying sluggishly under his stock of liquor. Right then I could have done with assistance.

They got me down in a corner. You can't fight three men of close upon your own size, and not go under in the end. Mustapha was no fighter himself, though the most dangerous because of the knife he carried, but those other two were toughies who had come up the hard way. They could take any amount of punishment and come back for more.

They came back once too often, and then I couldn't give them punishment.

They got me down, sprawling over me, panting, the blood trickling from the gashes I'd made on their sweating faces.

I just didn't have the strength now to throw them off, and Mustapha was trying to get between them, his eyes rolling as though he were mad, and that sharp knife feeling for a point in my ribs where it wouldn't do me any good.

I kicked and thrashed my body about, and that threw them off for a second, but then they were swarming back over me and this time there was no mistake about it — this time was it.

Mustapha had the knife pressed right up to my torn shirt. Then the door came down off its hinges — came flat down into the room under the weight of a mighty charge.

I could just see over Mustapha's shoulder, and when that door began to collapse, my thought was, *Baby's getting mad!*

But it wasn't Baby. I saw uniforms. They weren't uniforms I always care to see, but right then, I'd never seen a more wonderful colour in my life.

I saw cops come tumbling into that room, and even then Mustapha was trying to get the knife between my ribs. He knew it was his last chance.

But a big rangy cop slapped out with a hand like a ham and caught Mustapha on the side of his neck and sent him spinning off me.

Mustapha knew things were over with him. He'd been caught trying to remove a witness, and he figured there weren't many people going to believe him now.

We saw him jump for a window that had been smashed in the fighting, but he didn't get through. That rangy cop lurched across the room and grabbed him by his neck and hurled him back on to the floor. It was the end of resistance from Mustapha Agloul.

I got to my feet. The cops were holding Mustapha and his bodyguard. They were a sorry-looking lot. Just about as sorry-looking as I was, I guess. That police officer was there with the party now, looking very smart and brightly intelligent.

I made a statement. He took it down and I signed it. That was the end of Mustapha Agloul, I thought. Then they took the prisoners down the stairs and we left the Armenian to wonder what had hit his room when he came to.

Out on the landing, Baby was standing and smiling at me. I gave her a nip to her chin. A nice chin. A nice gal. Pity there was so much of her, I was thinking.

I said, 'Baby, for what you did you'll get two new dresses. Maybe three.' I was getting reckless. It was good to feel I had won through, and now I could live like a normal man again and not fear for my life.

She got it. She was amazing, the way

she understood with only a vocabulary of one word of English.

As I descended the steps she called down after me, 'Nylons?'

I said, 'Nylons, Baby.' Then I went down with the police into a square that had been cleared of fighting demonstrators. I got into a police car and no one tried to take a poke at me.

They dropped me at the hotel. I was quite a sensation, walking in. They saw me, a much-battered man, with a suit that wasn't good for anything except the ragbag.

The boys — Marty, Dwight, Tony and the others — nearly fell from their stools at the high bar when I came in. I got round a drink quickly.

I was boastful. I told them I had bust up this trouble like I'd bust up all other troubles that had come to Gissenheim's projects. They were nice guys and didn't tell me I'd brought the trouble on myself in the first place.

I went up to my room. My blood was pounding through my veins again. I wasn't even tired, suddenly.

I'd go into my room and have a shower and put on a new suit and then I'd get my lovely Rumanian and take her to the Gazino, or some other nightspot.

Right outside my door I halted as I saw another door open along from me. I knew whose door it was. The little Englishwoman's.

I saw her come out on to the carpeted corridor, that was so luxurious after the bare passages of the Armenian's dwelling. She stepped out brightly, a neat little woman who was more shapely than first impressions gave you. Quite a compact little woman, and not as old as I thought.

I snapped my fingers. After last night she was maybe feeling very young. That's how it affected women, often . . .

I gawked.

B.G. was coming out of the room behind her. I just stared at him. B.G. coming out of any woman's room!

He was walking aggressively, with his chest out and his fat chin held high.

Then he saw me, and he seemed to become deflated and uneasy. He knew the Heggy tongue could be cutting with sarcasm.

I gave the best Heggy grin a sore face could muster. I said, 'You two birds seem to be fraternising quite a lot.'

B.G. flushed, and little Lav dropped her eyes and seemed to flutter with embarrassment.

Then B.G. glared at me, defying me to contradict him. He said, 'Joe, I want you to know that we're both sorry for what happened last night.'

I was looking at little Lav. I didn't see any signs of sorrow on that demure little face. In fact all I could think of then was that a cat looked mighty like Lavinia when it had had its quota of milk.

But B.G. was going resolutely through with his story. 'It was the alcohol that did it. I've sworn off alcohol for evermore.' He was bracing himself again, believing what he said, the sucker. 'Miss Dunkley and I have agreed to continue to be friends, but our friendship must be on a purely platonic plane.'

I looked at him, and I thought he got crazier the older be got. Because one look at Lavinia told you she'd got plenty of ideas into her not-so-young head, and none of them was platonic.

I stood aside and they walked past me to an elevator that probably wouldn't work. I thought: I'll wait and see what happens when the moon comes up. This moon seemed to have a powerful effect upon the suppressed little Englishwoman.

Then I forgot them as I took a shower. They could work out their own future.

A little while later, refreshed and changed, I tapped on the Rumanian girl's door. She called a word in her own language, but I knew it meant, 'Come in.'

I went in.

With a girl like that, wouldn't you?

## THE END